T
of
Dark

Book 1

Journey to Zero

The Matter of Dark

a trilogy by Colin Stewart

Book I Journey to Zero

Book II Strangers and Adventurers

Book III The Ashes of Stars

a story of mystery, danger
... and the power of friendship

The Matter of Dark

Book 1

Journey to Zero

Colin Stewart

Elsbury Books

Illustrations by

Rachel Labovitch

First published in 2023 by
Elsbury Books, Studio 108820,
PO Box 4336, Manchester M61 0BW
elsburybooks@belerion.co.uk

All rights reserved
No part of this publication may be reproduced or transmitted by any means without the prior permission of the publisher

© Colin Stewart 2023
© Illustrations and Cover Artwork Rachel Labovitch 2023

The right of Colin Stewart to be identified as author of this work has been asserted in accordance with Section 77 of the Copyright, Designs and Patents Act 1988

A CIP catalogue record of this book is available from the British Library
ISBN 978-1-7392291-0-8

Typeset, printed and bound by Beamreach Printing, Cheshire

My Thanks to

Tom Jacobson
Tim Wilson
Sarah and Oscar Fitzharding
Neil Hall
Simon Wilson
Josh Lacey
Tony Audsley
Linda Davis
Rachel Labovitch
David Exley

for all their kind help with this book

Author's Note

In 1933, the astrophysicist Fritz Zwicky was studying the Coma cluster of galaxies. He discovered that the gravitational pull on the outer galaxies was much greater than it should have been for a cluster of that size. The strength of the gravity force depends on the amount of matter (mass) present and there just wasn't enough mass for that strong a pull. He suggested that there must be some invisible "Dark Matter" to make up the missing mass. For the next forty years, nobody really believed him.

Around 1970, a young astronomer called Vera Rubin pioneered a way to make more accurate measurements, and found that more than half of the mass of galaxies was undetectable except by its gravity. Not many people believed her, either.

But the great thing with science is that people keep chipping away at problems, so that either the evidence piles up to support an idea, or the theory gets knocked down and someone has to think up a better one.

A lot more evidence has since been collected to support the Dark Matter idea, and now nearly everybody believes it. The only surprise is that there is even more of it than first thought – around 95% of our Universe, in fact (although much of this may be in the form of Dark Energy rather than Dark Matter itself).

Nobody knows what Dark Matter is. There have been many suggestions. This book contains another one.

Chapter Zero

How did it get to this?

Awg lay on the bunk and stared straight up at the ceiling – or in the general direction of where he assumed any ceiling to be. In the dark it was hard to tell. At least the first cell had had a window. Looking through that had given him his first real indication that things were *definitely* not as they should be.

It had all started innocently enough. An accident. A journey to Wales. A walk up a mountain (well, part of the way up), though that *had* ended up with struggling through a graveyard at night and meeting a monk, who had then disappeared into thin air.

Since then he'd been knocked unconscious, imprisoned twice, nearly gnawed to the bone by rats – and was now facing interrogation, torture, and possibly death.

Perhaps if he went right back to the beginning and thought everything through very carefully, he could find out where it had all gone pear shaped.

Though of course there was still the bigger problem. Assuming he managed to survive the next few hours, how was he going to get back to Earth?

One

It was his dad's fault.

All of it. The whole works.

Everything.

What was the use of being a Genius Inventor if you just hadn't got any common sense?

Awg sat on the cold, hard station seat, drumming his heels against one of its metal supports.

Now he wasn't going to have a long summer holiday mucking around with his mates, kicking a ball about, laughing and joking, making a bike trail up in the quarry.

He was being Sent Away.

His mum would enjoy having an invalid in the house. She liked fussing round. It was bad enough when his dad was well: he got waited on hand and foot, so that he didn't have to worry about everyday things like getting meals and generally keeping the house running. His mum insisted that a genius should be free of such cares in order to nurture 'that precious creative spark.'

Perhaps that was why most of his inventions never worked. To be fair, they worked in a technical sense – the lights came on or the wheels went round – but there was almost always a *fatal flaw*.

The Humane Easy-Releasing Rat Trap was a success at first. But the rats soon learned to press the catch which opened the release door and let themselves out again. Sales declined.

The Self-Coiling Garden Hose worked brilliantly. Unfortunately, several people had to be taken to their local Fire

Stations to be cut free. They'd stood just a *little* bit too close when they pressed the button.

Awg gave the seat an especially hard kick, hoping to put a dent in it. But he knew he wouldn't. He knew all there was to know about that sort of seat. He should do – it paid for his existence. It was his father's only really successful invention.

The Bradley Patent Utility Bench was made entirely of rigid metal with a bare, weatherproof seat. It could be bolted to the ground and was virtually indestructible. Economical to manufacture but strong and vandal-proof, it was a runaway success. Now, you saw them everywhere.

But, strangely, you didn't often see people sitting on them. This was because of the fatal flaw. They were hideously uncomfortable. Awg was sitting on his rolled-up anorak – and under that were two thick newspapers he'd scrounged from the bin in the waiting room. *He* knew.

Awg gave the seat another hard kick. How could someone so clever be so stupid?

It was all his dad's fault.

Everything.

Two

Allardyce Wentworth Gilhooley Bradley was being sent away to stay with his grandmother. His dad had got the idea that the birds in his garden could read. And that was why he had fallen out of a tree and broken his arm.

Awg heard a train approaching and got up. He swung his bag over his shoulder. But it was the wrong train. This one was coming *from* Shrewsbury and he was going *to* Shrewsbury. He gave the seat another kick and sat down again. He knew his dad wasn't really a nutter – but he wished he didn't sometimes behave like one. Awg wondered what he was going to tell his grandmother. The truth was so mega-embarrassing.

It had started with a new idea for an ultrasonic bird-scarer. His dad made a thing like a notice-board on a pole and stuck it in the ground. He was going to fix the scarer to the board at the top. But he was still making last-minute improvements to the electronics, so it wasn't quite ready. To relieve his frustration, he wrote a big red notice and fixed it to the board. This is what it said:

NOTICE TO THE BIRDS IN THIS GARDEN
Stop eating my fruit and vegetables! Buzz off!!

He put the notice up on a Tuesday.

On Wednesday, he still hadn't finished the improvements – but he had decided that the pole was in the wrong place for maximum ultrasonic effect and moved the whole thing to the middle of the garden.

On Thursday, he still hadn't finished the improvements, but changed his mind again about where the pole should be and moved it all down to the bottom hedge.

On Friday, he still hadn't finished the improvements, but moved the pole back to the middle of the garden.

On Saturday, he still hadn't finished the improvements and was just going to move the pole and board (still carrying the notice) to *definitely the correct spot* by the water tap – when he suddenly realised that the birds hadn't raided anything in the garden since Tuesday. He then had a Eureka moment. It was obvious that the birds could read! The electrical scarer wasn't necessary! All you had to do was to put up a sign telling them what to do!

He explained this to some of his friends down at the Cordwainer's Arms the same evening. It is fair to say that they were not convinced. It is also fair to report that when he slipped out for a comfort break, they agreed among themselves that Barmy Bradley had moved on from mildly freaky to definitely barking.

Mr Bradley could see that further action was required to prove his point. He wrote out another notice:

NOTICE TO THE BIRDS IN THIS GARDEN
Please refrain from singing so early in the morning.
I suggest that you do not begin your dawn chorus
before 8 am (08.00 h)

He set up a tape recorder in one of the back rooms and poked the microphone out of the window. He rigged up a time switch that linked the recording on the tape to the time of day. That should be proof enough to convince the doubters. Then he got out a ladder so that he could fix the notice to the tallest place in the garden.

Then he fell out of the tree and broke his arm.

Three

Of course, the Allardyce Wentworth Gilhooley bit was his father's fault as well. They were the names of obscure inventors that he admired. 'A sort of dedication' he had said to his wife when their baby son was born. She never queried any of his suggestions.

Awg signed his name AWG Bradley, so everyone (except his parents) called him Awg. It wasn't the coolest of names, but it was a lot better than Allardyce, or Wentworth, or (especially) Gilhooley. It was bad enough being named after a bunch of losers without being constantly reminded of it.

Allardyce Wentworth Gilhooley
His dad's a raving loony

That's what the other kids used to chant at primary school. It could have been much worse at Brayhill Secondary, but it wasn't.

Because it was Awg who vanquished Skinner.

Skinner was a typical bully, and did all the things that typical bullies do. He robbed cash from the weaker kids. He got their glasses off them and stamped on them or threw them in the river. He stole stuff and sold it. He smashed people's faces in if they crossed him, or sometimes just for the fun of it even if they didn't. He went round with a gang of cronies who did the same things, when he let them. He'd been given warnings but Skinner ignored them. At least two of the teachers were as scared of him as the kids were. He was out of control.

Awg was not usually bothered by Skinner. This was mainly

because he didn't have stuff that Skinner wanted. At least not until last Christmas.

Awg sometimes wondered if his parents knew he was there at all, they took so little notice of him. If his dad as much as sniffed, he would be whisked off to bed and his mum would send for the doctor. But when Awg had got into a fight and come home with his shirt torn and blood and bruises all over his face, his mum had said, 'You do look a mess, dear. You'd better go upstairs and clean yourself up.'

So when he'd pointed out that his football boots were totally worn out, and too small for him anyway, he didn't expect much response. But, amazingly, his dad had taken him down to Evans Sports there and then and bought new ones. Not only that, he'd bought the best and most expensive ones in the shop. It made Awg's Christmas.

On the fateful day, Awg had been on his way to the football field next to the school. His new boots were strung around his neck by the laces. He'd changed into his soccer kit but kept his trainers on because there was no direct way into the field from the school. You had to go out of the school gate and along the pavement between a high fence and the road until you came to the corner. A little way around the corner the fence stopped and there was a gate into the field. And between Awg and the gate was Skinner and his gang.

'I'll take them boots, *Allardyce*.'

'D'yer gettem from yer loony dad?'

'Bet the studs'll drop out if he made 'em, Hahahahahaha.'

Skinner was sixteen years old and huge. Four of his mates were with him. Five against one.

Awg considered legging it.

Hopeless. Whatever happened, he was going to get damaged. But he was also hopping mad.

'Piss off, Skinner. If you want my boots, you'll have to go and get them!'

Awg hurled the boots over the fence. One of Skinner's henchmen ran into the field to where they lay on the grass. He was about to pick them up when Skinner lumbered through the gate towards him.

'Them boots is mine. Get yer thievin' hands off 'em.'

The rest of the gang watched to see what would happen. Awg saw his chance. He shot past them and into the field. A well-placed kick up Skinner's arse sent him sprawling into his mate. Awg scooped up his boots and ran past the tangle of arms and legs and away down the field. After a few moments he glanced back and saw five masses of concentrated hate zooming towards him. Things were serious.

The reason there was no direct way into the field from the school was because of the boundary dispute. Between the two was a strip of land on which stood the ruins of Nicholson's jam factory. The local council believed that they had bought the plot but the last survivor of the Nicholson family disagreed. Court proceedings had dragged on for years. To prevent the authorities sneaking in and taking possession when no one was looking, old Sammy Nicholson had settled on the site in a broken-down caravan, accompanied by three Rottweilers. No one trespassed.

Between the school and the football field, a twenty foot high wall marked the far end of the jam factory site. It was to the field end of this wall that Awg was now – desperately – running. But there was no way out at the bottom of the football field: it backed on to the river.

Awg was cornered. With the boots slung around his neck, he climbed up the links of the field fence and on to the end of the wall. Below, five people were waiting to kill him. They knew he had to come down, because there was nowhere else for him to go.

At its very top, the wall was only one brick wide. Nine inches. Exactly wide enough to stand on with your feet tight together and no space left over.

Awg took a few steps along the wall. He was terrified.

He stopped and looked around. Down to his left – twenty feet down – was the tangle of brambles, sagging walls and broken glass that had been the jam factory. He could just see old

Sammy's caravan with the dogs stretched out by the side. Down to his right, the ground fell away steeply to the river. Ahead of him was 30 yards of wall, one brick wide; at the end of it, the roof of the geography hut, and safety.

Gradually, although the fear was still there, a feeling was growing that he could do it. Somewhere, and somehow, he had the ability, if he could only keep his nerve. He turned to face his pursuers.

'OK Skinner, I'm going to walk back to the school. I dare you to follow me.'

And, turning again, and with his arms outstretched, he began to walk slowly along the wall.

Skinner and the gang stood and gaped in disbelief.

Awg did not stop, or glance back, or look down. He just walked, slowly, with his eyes on the target.

It took him about a minute, but he made it.

Skinner wasn't so lucky. He couldn't chicken out, with four of his gang looking on. So, to do him credit, he did try.

He got about a quarter of the way along before he fell. The bricks and broken glass didn't do him a lot of good – and then the Rottweilers got him. Sammy told the police he pulled them off almost at once, but it was suspected that he let them have a good chew first. Skinner and his cronies had persecuted the old man and made his life a misery. The doctors did their best for Skinner but agreed he would be scarred for life. He never went back to the school.

Four

This time, it was the right train, the one going *to* Shrewsbury. When he got there, Awg had to wait nearly two hours for a cross-country train that went down through the middle of Wales. The countryside was fairly flat when they started but it soon got wilder and much more hilly. The journey took ages and it was late in the day when he got to Pontrhyd.

There were two old women on the platform. Presumably, one was his gran. He couldn't remember what she looked like because she'd only visited them once, and that was a long time ago.

He went up to the nearest woman.

'Hello, I'm … Allardyce (it hurt him to say it). Are you Mrs Bradley?'

She looked surprised. 'Indeed I am not. The very idea!'

And she walked away.

He tried the other woman, who, by simple elimination, had to be the one.

'Hi, I'm Allardyce.'

'And so?'

'Aren't you my gran?'

'Not as far as I know. I have only one grandson, and he is in Canada.'

She smiled. 'What is your grandmother's name? Perhaps I know her.'

'It's Mrs Annie Bradley.'

'No, I cannot recall anyone of that name here.'

Awg dug in his pocket and fished out the envelope his mum had written.

Mrs Annie Bradley
Bryn Castell
Llangarreg
Pontrhyd

'Ah, it is Llangarreg that you are wanting, then.'

'Isn't that here?'

'No, it is up on Gellyn mountain. I think there is a bus from the stop outside the station.'

Awg thanked her and picked up his bag.

He soon found the bus stop. There was a map and the times of buses going to three different places. The entry for Llangarreg was very short:

Pontrhyd	10.05*	15.05*
Pen-y-gwyn	10.14*	15.14*
Llangarreg (Priory)	10.19*	15.19*

* Thursdays only

The bus would have gone hours ago – and anyway today was Monday.

Across the street was a small shop, which was still open. Awg went inside and bought a bag of peppermints as emergency rations. He had eaten the last of his sandwiches on the train. Then he had a closer look at the notice on the bus stop.

Pontrhyd to Llangarreg takes the bus fourteen minutes. That's about a quarter of an hour. It'll be narrow lanes so it can't go very fast, so say 25 mph. So it's a quarter of 25, which is about six miles.

'Quite right. It is six and a half miles from here to Llangarreg.'

Awg jumped. He hadn't realised that he had been saying the words out loud. Not very loud, but enough for someone standing directly behind him to hear.

The man was about seventy, dressed in a tweed jacket and corduroy trousers tied up with string.

'I'm going up to Pen-y-gwyn, if that is any good to you.'

They got into a battered old Landrover and rattled off up the street. A black and white dog ran from side to side in the open back, barking as they rounded each corner. At the end of the town, they crossed a bridge and turned up a steep and narrow lane. The road twisted and climbed. At one place they went creaking and swinging round a hairpin bend with a waterfall crashing down at the side. After a few minutes, they pulled up in front of a cluster of stone farm buildings. The sun had disappeared behind the hills and it was beginning to get dark.

'Here's as far as I can take you.'

'Thanks a lot. Do I just keep along this road to get to Llangarreg?'

'Yes, the road will take you to Llangarreg. There is also the field path: the Abbot's Way they call it. It is shorter in distance – but it goes through the Priory itself, so you should not take it.'

'Why ever not, if it's quicker?'

The man stared at him.

'I did not say that it was quicker – or safer. Only that it was shorter in distance.'

'Perhaps if I went by the road, someone might come along who would give me a lift?'

'No one will be going up to Llangarreg at this hour.'

'But it's not late, it's only just after eight o'clock.'

'I am telling you, there is no one here who will go to Llangarreg after dark.'

Five

Awg swung down from the Landrover and set off briskly up the road. From the bus timetable, he knew that he still had at least two miles to walk. He had best stick to the road. No sense getting lost taking short cuts.

He wondered why his gran had not come down to meet him. And what did the farmer mean about no one wanting to go to Llangarreg after dark?

The lane continued to climb steeply. The hedges at the side were very overgrown and the road surface was deteriorating rapidly. There were frequent potholes, and clumps of grass growing along the middle.

He stopped at a gateway for a breather. He was about to move on when he saw a small, wooden footpath sign: *Llangarreg 1 mile*. It was very tempting. Surely he couldn't go far wrong in a mile?

He left the lane and struck off up the path. After crossing two fields, the track bore steeply downwards and entered a wood. It became very marshy underfoot and Awg heard the sound of running water. He rounded a corner and found himself at the bank of a fast-flowing stream. It looked deep and there was no way across. So much for short cuts!

He began to make his way upstream, stumbling over branches and tree roots. At least this was in the same general direction that he had been going before, and he might find some way to cross the stream.

Before long he came to another wooden signpost – in the failing light he almost walked into it – and just a few yards farther on was a very old bridge. Stone uprights had been set into the bed of the stream and across these were laid flat stone slabs held together with iron straps. A clear track led away on either side. Somewhere, he must have diverged from the proper path, probably just before that marshy bit.

Thankfully, he crossed the bridge. The path still led uphill but was gradually getting less steep.

Now he was passing under an avenue of huge and ancient trees. Against the darkening sky an arch of stone reared over his head, and suddenly he was in the Priory itself. Awg caught his breath, and for the first time began to feel scared. Everything was wildly overgrown. Trailing creepers brushed his shoulder. All around were fallen blocks of stone, crumbling walls, the remains of stone arches. Tombs and gravestones canted over at unnatural angles, throwing crazed shadows over the tangle of undergrowth. And somewhere, in the distance, a light was burning.

Awg made his way cautiously along the outside of a low wall until he came to a small building which was much more complete than the rest. There were four walls and most of the roof. The light was coming from the stone doorway. Awg crossed the grass and went inside.

At the far end of the building was a three-arched window. Below this, a small stone cross stood on a granite altar. In a recess at the side were a candle and an hourglass. In front of these sat a monk.

'Uh – Hello,' said Awg.

The monk turned slowly to face him. He spoke in a thin, tired voice.

'I was hoping there was no one about.'

'Sorry,' said Awg.

'Are you going to scream and run around in circles waving your arms?'

'No, why should I?' said Awg.

'It's just that's what most of them do. It's terribly upsetting. I do try to keep out of the way as much as possible. Are you new here?'

'Yes.'

'I thought so. Sensible.'

'I've come to stay with my grandmother, Mrs Bradley, only I haven't managed to find her yet. I got a bit lost.'

'Ummmm. Annie Bradley. Well, you've found her.'

'You mean, she lives *here*.'

'Yes. Well, not here exactly. In the castle.'

'The castle?'

'That's what they call it, now. Bryn Castell – the castle on the mound. It's just a house, really. It *was* a castle once, then it became part of the Priory. Then the Priory was destroyed and the oldest part was made into a house. I lived in it myself, a long time ago. That was when I was doing the clocks. Oh dear!'

He had caught sight of the hourglass, the sand in which had almost completely run through.

'I've got to go now. Sorry. I'll leave the candle for you so that you can see your way out. Please don't mention anything about this to your grandmother: no sense in worrying her. Oh, my name's Benedict, by the way. Nice to meet you. 'Bye.'

The candle burned beside the altar.

The last grains of sand ran out.

The monk and the hourglass vanished.

Six

Unlike his brilliant but nutty father, Awg had a plentiful supply of common sense.

It did not, for example, take him very long to work out that if you put up a large and colourful notice in the middle of your garden, it will act as a scarecrow and keep the birds off for a few days. Especially if you keep moving it about from one part of the garden to another. All that reading stuff was a load of cobblers.

So when the monk and his hourglass vanished into thin air, Awg took a few moments to recover from the shock – but then very quickly began to look around to discover where he could have gone. As far as he could see, there was no trap door into which he might have jumped, and the altar and wall appeared totally solid. Nothing could have whisked him up into the air and the idea of some elaborate hoax with lasers and mirrors seemed out of the question.

Besides, the monk had vanished. Not got up and walked out. Not slipped to one side. Not gradually faded away. *Vanished.* He was there one second and gone the next.

The monk had been a ghost, then.

No, he had looked far too solid for that and his conversation had been too matter-of-fact. If he had been a proper ghost, at least he might have looked a bit luminous or shimmery, and wittered on about being the spirit of your poor dead uncle, or something. He was a perfectly ordinary monk – who just happened to disappear into thin air.

????????????????????????

Awg had a sudden idea and rushed over to the alcove where the candle still burned. By its side, he could see a ring in the dust where the hourglass had stood. So it had been a real hourglass. And he was sure that the monk had been real as well.

So where had he gone?

Awg picked up the candle and used it to light his way to the door. He checked the building inside and out, and there was definitely no one else about. He blew out the candle and placed it carefully in his pocket.

There was a half-moon, and enough light from the sky for him to re-find the path. After a few moments he came to a gate in a hedge and went through into a lane. Probably the one down to Pen-y-gwyn, he thought. If he'd stayed on the road this is where he would have finished up. But then he'd never have met the monk.

Awg could see a number of buildings farther down the lane but he was now heading away from them and towards a house on its own on the priory side of the road. His heart leapt when he saw it, for this was no ordinary house. This was a castle. A small one, admittedly, but a castle true enough – a round tower with a castellated top, and the flag of Wales flying from its roof.

He opened the garden gate and walked up the path. The tall, narrow windows were shuttered but there was a light inside, so someone was at home. On a stone tablet over the front door were carved the letters

Bryn Castell
I Dduw y bo'r Diolch

Awg knocked at the door. After what seemed a very long time, a heavy lock was turned and several bolts were drawn back.

A tiny woman with a mass of silver hair stood at the door. In her hand she brandished an iron poker.

'Who on earth are you?' she said. 'And what do you want at this time of night?'

Seven

Awg stared at the silver-haired woman. He could see she was cross at being disturbed. Perhaps this one wasn't his gran, either.

He also felt rather uneasy about the poker.

'Are you from the travellers?' said the woman. 'Are you from the Television?'

Awg was at a loss to know what he should say.

'My name's Allardyce Bradley. I'm not from the TV or anything. Are you my gran?'

The woman's jaw dropped and she put her hand to her head. She also lowered the poker.

'Good Gracious! You're Thomas's boy. Come in, come in.'

Awg picked up his bag and followed his grandmother into the house. The room in which he found himself was completely circular. It looked welcoming and comfortable and a fire was burning in the grate. On the walls, on tables, on shelves and on the mantelpiece were a total of twenty-six clocks (he counted them later).

'I ... I don't think you were expecting me,' said Awg.

'No indeed. No, indeed. My Goodness!'

'So mum didn't tell you I was coming – or ask you if I could stay?'

'No. Not a word. Not a syllable. No letter. No phone call. Typical!'

Awg took out the envelope his mother had given him and handed it to his grandmother.

She opened the letter. This is what it said:

Dear Granny Bradley

I am sending Allardyce to stay with you as I have to devote all my energies to caring for my darling Thomas who has broken his arm. I am sure you will be glad of the company since you lost poor dear Grandpa.

Affectionately yours
Amelia

'Typical!' said his grandmother. 'Typical!

'When Thomas met your mother, I could see it all. She'd coddle him and spoil him and let him have his way with everything, and that's just what happened. I gave up on them years ago.'

Her face softened into a wry smile.

'Still, she does look after him and I daresay that no one else would put up with all his nonsense. It still amazes me that they were organised enough to produce a child at all.'

She let her spectacles slide down her nose and stared at him over the top.

'Well, now you're here, you're here. At least you look as though you might have a bit more gumption than your father. I've no time to set up a bed for you, so you'll have to sleep on the sofa tonight. Now, when did you last have a proper meal?'

Awg cast his mind back over a hurried breakfast of toast and a lunch of railway sandwiches.

'About six o'clock yesterday evening, I think.'

'Good Gracious! Not content with sending their children off unannounced to the wilds of Wales, they starve them to death as well. Typical!'

She disappeared through a door at the back of the room. In about a minute she was back.

'You'll have to wait a little while, but I can get you vegetable soup, steak pie with jacket potatoes, apple crumble and custard. Will that do?'

Awg replied that it would do very well indeed.

Eight

Daylight streamed through the shutters and there were birds singing. Awg felt deliciously warm and snug. He was almost submerged under a pile of quilts and eiderdowns. But it was definitely time to get up. There was the smell of breakfast cooking.

His gran's head appeared at the door.

'I've put your things in the top room. There's a water jug and basin, so tidy yourself up and come down when you're ready. Do you like bacon, eggs, sausages and things like that?'

For a moment, Awg wondered if he'd died and gone to heaven. At home, he was used to getting his own breakfast of cornflakes and toast. He extracted himself from the cocoon of improvised bedclothes and trotted about looking for some stairs. Around him, the twenty-six clocks ticked away like crickets on a summer morning.

There were three doors in the strange, round room. There was the front door, by which he had come in last night; a door at the back of the room, which he knew must lead to the kitchen; and a further door with a rounded top in the wall opposite the fireplace. He lifted the latch and found himself in a narrow space with whitewashed stone steps leading upwards to his right. He realised that he was *inside* the wall of the tower.

Half way up was a stone landing, where a slit window brightened the shadowy space. From here, another arched door opened into a room on the middle floor. Awg guessed that this was his gran's bedroom.

He continued up the narrow stairs to the top and a third

arched door. He opened it and found himself in the uppermost room of the castle. Light flooded in from four tall windows. He rushed across – and gasped at the view. It seemed to him that he was looking out over the whole of Wales.

The air in the room was fresh and clean but carried a faint smell of wood shavings and machine oil. Under one of the windows a space had been cleared for a folding bed, table and washstand. But these were obviously recent additions. The room wasn't intended as a bedroom.

Most of the area was occupied by a large wooden workbench, a rack of unusual-looking tools and a small lathe. Parts of clocks lay neatly arranged inside a large open box, the interior of which was divided up into small compartments, and an unfinished clock-case stood by the side. On the wall were shelves of books. Awg took down a few volumes that he could reach. *A Clockmaker's Almanack. Watches: Adjustment and Repair. Robert Hooke and the Anchor Escapement. The Metal Turner's Handbook.* Each one had the same name inside, written neatly on the flyleaf in black ink: Joseph Bradley.

Awg took the jug and half-filled the basin. The water was a peaty colour and had brown bits in the bottom. He stuck his head into the basin, gave his face a good rub and then pulled a comb a few times through his wiry hair. That would do. He went downstairs and found his gran in the kitchen cooking breakfast on a huge black stove. She settled down to toast and marmalade while Awg wolfed down a large plate of bacon and eggs.

'Shall I call you Gran?' asked Awg.

'Yes, if you like. It's short and to the point. But what am I going to call you? Allardyce?'

'Please, no!'

'What do your friends call you?'

'Awg.'

'I see, from your initials. Awg it shall be, then.'

His grandmother poured herself a second cup of tea.

'Now, Awg, you must understand that I live very simply here.

Water comes from the pump in the kitchen, vegetables and fruit from my garden and eggs from my hens. Every Thursday I go down on the bus to the market in Pontrhyd to get the other household things I need.'

She looked at Awg very intently over the top of her spectacles.

'So, if you're going to be here with me for a while – and you are very welcome I may add – then you must help me in the house and in the garden. Each day, there will be things to do. Of course, when you have finished your jobs, you are free to go wherever you wish. I'm sure you can take care of yourself and you will find many interesting places on Gellyn mountain to discover and explore.'

There were loads of things Awg was dying to ask his grandmother but he didn't want to seem too inquisitive, especially at first. He would have to find out a few things at a time.

'Gran …'

'Yes, Awg.'

'When I came up here yesterday, I got a lift from a farmer as far as Pen-y-gwyn.'

'That would be Edward Pryce, I expect.'

'Well, he said a funny thing.'

'Yes?'

'When I asked him if anyone would be driving up to Llangarreg he said that no one would go up there after dark.'

'Did he indeed! Well, now – you mustn't believe all you hear.'

'Yes, but what did he mean?'

'I suppose there's no harm in telling you that Llangarreg has something of a reputation. Odd happenings, UFO sightings and so on. We get hippies camping out in the fields, especially at the summer solstice, and the television people are always up here nosing around for a story. Most of it's a load of nonsense but the local folk are very touchy about it. They think it all goes back to when the monks were here the first time.'

'The *first time?*'

'When the Priory was in its heyday. The monks first settled

here in 1115 and they stayed for four centuries – until the dissolution of the monasteries. Do you know about that?'

'It was Henry VIII, wasn't it? He had them knocked down and pocketed all their money.'

'That's right. The small and remote ones like Llangarreg were the last to go. The king's men came and destroyed our buildings in 1542.'

'But the monks came back?'

'Yes, their Order survived the dissolution. Many generations later, a monk called Brother Benedict returned with three lay workers. They rebuilt the chapel and part of the old castle and established themselves in the village. Did you notice their inscription above the front door as you came in? *I Dduw y bo'r Diolch*. That's "God be Praised" in the Old Welsh.'

Awg nodded. He'd wondered what it meant – and when it had been written.

'In those latter days they had to make their own living,' continued his grandmother, 'and so they adopted the profession of clockmakers. Llangarreg clocks became quite famous and that was why Grandpa Joseph wanted to settle here when he retired.'

'Gran ...'

'*Yes*, Awg?'

'You said it was many years later that Benedict lived here. Do you mean, quite recently?'

'Well, comparatively recently, certainly.'

'But when, exactly?'

'As far as I can remember, they finished making clocks here in 1776.'

Nine

Awg fed the chickens and pumped up several buckets of water for his gran to use in the kitchen. You opened a big brass tap at the sink and worked a long iron handle at the side. After a few seconds, a gush of water came out of the tap – but it stopped as soon as you stopped pumping.

That was all for the moment, so he slipped out of the garden gate and made his way down to the Priory. In the daylight, it didn't look at all scary, just a rather forlorn and beautiful ruin. He went into the little chapel, and found the altar and the cross just as they had been the night he arrived. He searched very carefully to see if there was a crypt or any sort of cellar or vault under the floor, but he could find nothing. It all looked very ordinary.

He took the candle out of his pocket and placed it in the recess where it had been before. Benedict might need it if he came back.

If he came back.

If he came back from where?

Something from yesterday's conversation with his grandmother had stuck in Awg's mind. When they were talking about the reports of odd goings-on in Llangarreg she had said 'Most of it's a load of nonsense'. *Most* of it. That sounded as if there were *some* things that she thought might be true, and he knew his grandmother was not given to flights of fancy. He wondered if she herself had seen something – or someone.

Awg shook off the chill of the chapel's shadows and went outside into the sunshine. The castle and the priory were very close to one another and it was obvious that they had once been part of the same group of buildings. Awg looked up at the tower to identify which windows belonged to his room. If he could see his bedroom windows from outside the chapel, then he must be able to see the chapel from his windows. He decided to keep watch.

Each time he had to go up to his room for any reason, Awg got into the habit of taking a quick glance from the window to look out for anything unusual. He checked last thing at night and again first thing in the morning. If he woke in the night, he padded quickly over the cold wooden floor to the window and surveyed the priory grounds, always so different at night: mysterious by starlight, really spooky in moonlight.

Once he saw a fox scurrying along the path, then rooting and snuffling in the bushes.

Then one morning he woke very early, just before dawn, and there was a light in the chapel. It was very faint, but he could see it shining through one of the side windows and there was a faltering glow from the door.

Awg pulled on his tracksuit and crept down the stairs, very quietly – the last thing he wanted was to wake his grandmother and alarm her. It took him what seemed an age to slide the bolts on the great front door and turn the heavy key in its lock. Then he was running down the lane, slipping through the gate into the Priory, stealing noiselessly along the path to the chapel.

And everything was in darkness.

He passed silently through the stone gateway and stood, trembling, in the blackness. Nothing moved. The only sound was the thumping of his own heart. He took his torch from his pocket, held his breath and turned it on. He swept the narrow beam around the vaulted space, probing every corner. His mouth dry, he crept up to the altar and shone his torch into the recess at the side. There was a new ring in the dust where the hourglass had stood before, and the candle was gone.

Ten

Awg couldn't find a stepladder.

He'd got up on a chair and was just about to balance one foot on the back to stretch just that little bit higher when his grandmother came in.

'Awg – I don't think that's a very good idea ...

'... And anyway, it isn't necessary.'

Awg unbalanced himself and stepped down. He'd been given the job of winding all the clocks. There were round clocks and square clocks, modern clocks and very old clocks. There were brass clocks and china clocks and clocks made from every sort of wood. Tall grandfather clocks stood stiffly against the wall, frowning sternly at the diminutive carriage clocks on their low shelves.

Some needed winding every day, others only once a week. There were twenty-six in the main room, eleven in the kitchen and another eighteen in his grandmother's bedroom. The keys for the clocks in each room were kept in separate boxes, and, after he'd worked out which key fitted each clock, Awg had soon wound them all.

Except one.

On a high shelf in the main room was a clock he couldn't reach.

'You don't need to wind that one,' said his grandmother.

'Why not?' asked Awg.

'Because it never needs winding.'

'You mean – it doesn't need winding very often?'

'No, I mean it never needs winding.'

She smiled at Awg's puzzled expression and handed him a wooden basket.

'We call that one the Old Curiosity. Now – come into the garden and help me pick some peas.'

Later on, when Awg did find a stepladder, he climbed up until he was level with the clock and had a good look at it.

He stared, mesmerised. On the shelf stood a clock unlike any other he had ever seen.

The case appeared to be made of wood, but it was absolutely jet black. Not a shiny black that reflected your face in it but a dull, anonymous black that seemed to absorb all the light that fell upon it. And it was triangular.

A black equilateral triangular block of side twelve inches (Awg could almost hear his maths teacher saying the words) and depth eight inches.

The round face of the clock was set dead in the centre of the triangle. The face was white with beautifully-scribed numerals in black.

But the thing that had sent the hairs prickling on the back of Awg's neck was just below the central spindle that held the delicate black hands of the clock.

Just about where you would expect the hole for the winding key to be, in fact.

Except there was no hole for a key.

Instead, there was the maker's name, and a date:

Benedict
Llangarreg
1747

Eleven

For the rest of the day, Awg couldn't take his mind off the strange triangular clock. At first, he had thought it to be completely silent. But if you listened really carefully, with your ear up close, you could hear the slow, gentle ticking of the mechanism: click … uhh … click … uhh … click … uhh … click …

At supper that evening, Awg decided to find out a bit more.

'Gran – why do you call it the Old Curiosity?' he asked.

'Because that's what it is – at least, according to your Grandpa Joseph.

'It was always his ambition to own an original Llangarreg clock but he couldn't ever get one. They're very rare and valuable.

'Then, when we came here, he found that one in the garden shed. It was in an awful state but – do you know – it was still going, actually ticking away. He did a lot to clean it up and restore it, but he could never quite fathom out exactly how it worked. He said it had a unique feature, whatever that was.'

'How could a clock like that be left in a garden shed?' asked Awg.

'It isn't known exactly where the monks made their clocks,' said his grandmother. 'We know that they lived in this house and worshipped in the Priory chapel. But we think that there were once other buildings – possibly their workshops – at the bottom of the garden.'

She went to the stove and returned with another helping of vegetables for Awg.

'You can see the remains of a few walls and some foundations. Perhaps the workshops were knocked down and the stone used for something else by the local farmers. But the people who lived here before us built a little shed up against one of the surviving walls, and it was in a space in that old back wall that Joseph found the clock. He discovered it when he was drilling some holes to put up a shelf. Suddenly the drill went through into nothing, and when he took away some old plaster he found that clock in the space.'

'Gran – that room I'm in ...'

'Yes, I'm sorry – but I've nowhere else to put you. There are only the three rooms and this little back kitchen.'

'No, it's not that. I like it. But what is it?'

'It was your grandad's workshop. That's where he made his clocks.

'We had a shop in Shrewsbury. He bought and sold clocks and did repairs but he never had the time to make a complete clock. But he was very interested in the old clockmakers and their craft. When he retired, he looked around for somewhere that had been famous for its clocks and so we sold the shop and came here. Then he had the time to start making clocks himself. He made six clocks in this house and signed them 'Joseph Bradley, Llangarreg' with the date. He was very proud of that. You'll see them amongst the rest of his collection as you go around on your winding duties.

'So your room is where those clocks were made. I've left things exactly as they were, just in case.'

'In case ... of what?'

'In case he comes back.'

'But mum told me that you lost him ten years ago.'

'Yes, that's right. Ten years ago on the thirtieth of July at a quarter past eleven in the morning.'

Awg felt that the conversation was taking a decidedly weird turn. He had no memory of his grandad at all, although he knew there was a photo of himself in his arms as a baby.

'I'm so sorry', said Awg. 'Had he been ill for long?'

'Oh, no. He wasn't ill at all.'

'So, was it an accident?'

'Yes, you could say that – in a manner of speaking.'

'How awful! Was he in pain?'

'No, not as far as I could tell. He just bent over, said "Well I never!" and that was that.'

'He died, just like that?'

'Oh, no. He didn't die.'

'Didn't die?'

'No, he disappeared. One minute he was sitting there, on the rock – and the next minute he wasn't. He just vanished.'

Twelve

Awg was thunderstruck. A disappearing monk was bad enough but a vanishing grandfather was just too much. He looked at his grandmother's face and saw that she'd gone very pale.

'When grandad disappeared – what did you do?' he whispered.

'I tried to tell myself that he'd just had an accident, so I scrambled around trying to find where he might have fallen. But I couldn't find anything, not a trace. And all the time I knew in myself that it was hopeless, because I was sure that he *hadn't* fallen. I was staring straight at him when he spoke, and he just disappeared into thin air.'

'So did you eventually just give up looking for him?' asked Awg.

'Yes. I went home and notified the police. They organised a search with dogs and a helicopter but they couldn't find anything, either. So Joseph has been added to the list of missing persons, "whereabouts unknown".

'I felt badly about all the time they spent, because I didn't tell them the whole truth. I told them we were out having a picnic together – and I was putting the sandwich boxes away – and when I looked up he wasn't there. Everything I said was the perfect truth, except that very last bit. I couldn't tell them I saw him vanish into thin air. They would have thought that I was weak in the head.'

She looked at him, and he saw fear in her eyes.

'Is that what *you* think, Awg?' she said.

Awg was in a terrible dilemma. His grandmother was

obviously near to tears. Should he tell her about the monk he'd seen, or would that upset her even more?

'No, gran. I believe you,' he said, at last. 'There's something weird about Llangarreg, I'm sure of it.'

She put her arm around him and gave him a hug.

'Everyone told me I should leave – that I should go to live somewhere else and make a new start. But I love it here. It's a beautiful place, and I have such happy memories of your grandpa.

'Besides, I feel somehow that if I did go away, he never would return; while if I stay, perhaps there's some chance that whatever happened might somehow reverse itself and he might come back to me.

'So here I am, a silly old woman with fond remembrances and just a little bit of hope. And it's lovely having you here, Awg – you're a real companion. You remind me of Joseph. I think you've got his kindness, and maybe his determination too.'

Thirteen

Awg had grown to like his grandmother very much. She was generous and kind but very down-to-earth and practical. A bigger contrast with his vague and cranky parents could hardly be imagined.

He'd got used to the idea that his grandfather was dead – and now it seemed that he wasn't. Awg didn't know whether to feel pleased or not. From a practical point of view, it didn't seem to make much difference: he wasn't ever going to meet him, or talk to him, or feel his hand on his shoulder.

But his grandmother hadn't given up hope, so perhaps he shouldn't either.

Awg tried to decide what he should do. The easiest thing would be to do nothing, and just enjoy his time at Llangarreg. He didn't know how long he was staying and he wanted to explore some of the places his grandmother had told him about. The top of Gellyn mountain, where you looked out along four different valleys and could see for thirty miles on a clear day. The path up to Ty Nant, where there was a cave behind a waterfall.

But, at the back of his mind, he knew that he was going to have to do some detective work, and the sooner he began, the better. He would continue to keep a watch on the chapel, but the chances of catching Benedict again seemed slim. Awg had a lot of things he wanted to ask that monk.

Apart from a disturbing tendency to vanish without warning, the thing that connected Benedict and his grandfather was the clocks – and one clock in particular. Something about its appearance was really unsettling, and it was not just the shape and the colour. Awg remembered watching a TV programme about the ancient Mayan civilisation in Central America. He had seen great pyramid temples in the jungle with flights of steps sweeping right up to their tops. There had been huge palaces with fantastic carvings and observatories with black stone monuments carrying hieroglyphic inscriptions. There was something about them that didn't seem to belong on this planet at all and he had the same sort of feeling about the clock.

Awg decided to have another look at it.

The case was completely smooth and had no markings of any kind on it. Awg edged it forward on the shelf. It was obviously very heavy. Lifting it down was going to be a project in itself. He slid it carefully back to its usual position and was just getting down off the steps when he saw something he hadn't noticed before. Just below the name and date on the face was another mark. It was small and rather faint. He ran up to his room to fetch the magnifying glass he had seen on his grandfather's workbench. Awg moved the lens to and fro in front of his eye. The mark expanded into a blob, and then resolved itself into a strange symbol, a bit like a child's drawing of the sun:

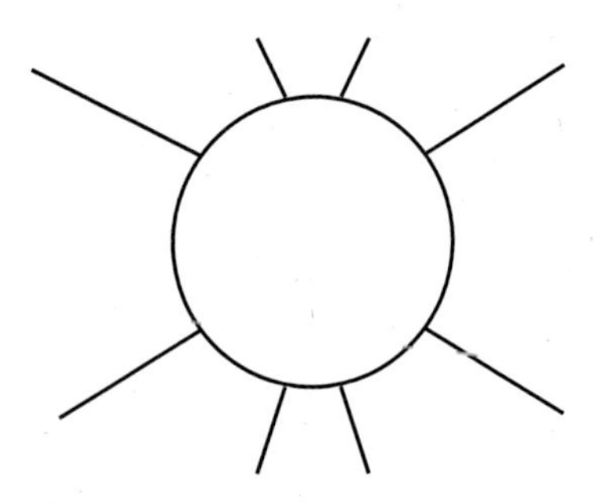

Awg made a little sketch of it, so that he wouldn't forget.

Over the next few days, Awg set about examining the other clocks. He hadn't looked at them too closely as he went round winding them each morning but now he had a reason for getting more interested. Many of the clocks had maker's names, and often dates, so that you knew who had constructed them, and when. Awg was especially proud of the six clocks that his grandfather had made, all skilfully crafted and signed 'Joseph Bradley, Llangarreg'.

One morning, Awg was winding the smallest of his grandfather's clocks. It was raining too hard to do much outside, so Awg decided to take the back off to see how it worked. He took the clock up to his workshop bedroom and placed it on the bench. Then he selected a small screwdriver from the collection in the rack and took out the screws. Awg was captivated by the beautiful mechanism he found inside. It moved so effortlessly and made such a satisfyingly busy sound: k'tick-click, k'tick-click, k'tick-click.

He looked along the rows of books on the wall and selected the simplest one he could find. It was obviously written for beginners so it was just right for him. He compared the drawings and description in the book with what he could see inside the clock. Awg didn't dare tinker with the mechanism itself in case he did something awful to it, but after an hour or two he had a pretty good idea of what sort of mechanism it was and how it worked.

By the end of the week, Awg had examined all six of his grandfather's clocks and was getting more confident in his understanding of them. He began to investigate the other timepieces in the house and to compare the very old clocks with some of the newer ones. He looked into some of the more complicated books and found he could now follow a lot of what was in them.

Awg began to study the half-completed clocks and trays of parts which were in the workroom. In one of the drawers in the bench he found a complete clock mechanism. He by now could recognise that this was a cheap, mass-produced modern movement of little value, and could only assume that his grandad had intended to use it as a pattern for something, or for spare parts. Over the course of the day, he took it completely to pieces, cleaned and oiled it, and put it together again. It wouldn't work at all and it took him a long time to discover the mistake he'd made in assembling it. However, he finally got it working, and after a few more slip-ups succeeded in adjusting it to keep reasonable time.

A few days later, one of the clocks in the kitchen stopped. It was an eight-day clock and wasn't due to be wound until the end of the week. When Awg came into the room his grandmother was in the process of giving the clock a good shake, but she couldn't get it to re-start. She was very surprised when Awg asked if he could try to mend it.

'I've been finding out a bit about clocks,' he explained. 'I've looked at some of grandad's books and some of the clock bits in my room. I think I might be able to do something.

'I'll be very careful,' he added hastily, seeing his gran's worried expression.

To his grandmother's amazement, he brought the clock back after supper, and it was going.

'It was easy. There was a tiny flake of wood caught in the escapement. I took it out with tweezers. I've cleaned inside the case, so it shouldn't happen again.'

That night, Awg's grandmother felt happier than she had for a long time. She felt that Joseph was somehow just a little nearer.

Sitting up in bed, Awg took out a book he'd found earlier in his search through the shelves: *The Welsh Clockmakers* by Henry Lloyd Lewis. He turned to the section on Central Wales.

Llangarreg

The Llangarreg workshop was unusual in that it was run entirely by a small group of monks and their lay associates. Their small manufactory operated from around 1732 until a disastrous fire in the year 1776 forced them to cease work. The Llangarreg clocks are noted for the excellence of their workmanship and the ingenuity of their construction. The most highly prized are those made by the founding father of the enterprise, Brother Benedict, of whose craftsmanship only eight examples are known to have survived. Of these, one is in the National Museum of Wales and one in the London Science Museum, whilst the remainder are in private collections. Benedict is known to have corresponded with leading contemporary horologists, notably Mudge and Graham, whilst a letter to John Harrison concerning the use of different metals to achieve temperature compensation was sold at Sotheby's in 1972 for an undisclosed sum, believed to be in excess of £5000.

Mystery surrounds the fate of Brother Benedict himself. Following the fire he disappeared, and there is a tradition that he perished in the flames. However, no trace of his body was ever discovered.

Awg padded downstairs to look at the triangular clock again. It wasn't every day you saw a clock that had run without winding for over two hundred years.

Fourteen

Awg had been watching *Crimescene* on the television and it had given him an idea. They would re-enact the day his grandfather disappeared. Tomorrow was July 30th – the tenth anniversary. Perhaps this might provide some clue as to what had happened.

The day was fine, his grandmother packed up some sandwiches and they set off for the top of the mountain.

'Are you sure you want to do exactly as we did on that day?' asked his grandmother.

Awg said yes he was sure, so they set off at half past nine, just as his grandmother and grandfather had done ten years before.

They started out by taking the path through the Priory. The sun played over the mossed stones and ivy-covered walls. There was no hint of mystery – or menace – as they walked along together.

'It's OK here at the moment,' said Awg, thinking back to his encounter with the monk, 'but it was a bit different the first night I came. It was scary – full of secrets and shadows.'

'Yes,' said his grandmother. 'You should have followed Edward Pryce's advice and kept to the road.'

'Gran –' said Awg.'You know what you said about Llangarreg – about it having a name for odd goings-on. What sort of stuff did you mean?'

'Well, there's stories about flying saucers and so on. That's not been going long and I think that most of it's made up. The only person *I* know who thought she'd seen anything was old Mrs Jones at Tyle-mawr. I think she'd heard about these UFO sightings and got a bit fanciful.

'She saw a flashing orange light moving backwards and forwards in mid air and called the police. But it turned out it was only a farmer on his tractor the other side of a hedge. He'd been trying to clear a drain that had overflowed in the middle of the night and flooded part of his farm.'

'But there's things that've been going on for longer?' asked Awg.

'Oh yes,' said his grandmother. 'Stories going back for hundreds of years. Mostly connected with the Priory – lights moving about and that sort of thing.'

'Just lights, not ... people?'

'Well, yes. There are reports of a monk walking in the grounds or in the chapel.'

'Do you believe it – have you ever seen anything yourself?'

'The way I look at it is this,' said his grandmother. 'Those monks were here for hundreds of years and they didn't leave of their own accord. They were expelled from land which was rightfully theirs, so perhaps something of their presence remains in some way. And, yes – I *have* sometimes seen lights in the Priory at night.'

They reached the stile at the far end of the Priory grounds.

'And I think it was here that your grandpa Joseph saw the monk.'

'What!' exclaimed Awg.

'We had a little dog, then, and Joseph used to take him out each evening. They'd usually go through the Priory, either in at the side gate and back down the road or the other way around. Well, this particular evening, Joseph was just coming up to this stile when he saw there was a man sitting on it: on the lower step – that one there. As he approached, the figure got up and Joseph saw it was a monk in his hood and habit. He gave a little bow to Joseph, who passed him by and climbed over the stile – but when he looked back there was no one there – no one at all.'

Once over the stile, they walked for a time along a narrow lane until it came to an end at two cottages. There, they turned off along an old forest road. Soon they crossed a stone bridge where the road divided. They took the left fork and continued through the trees, the track climbing gently all the while with the stream chattering down on their left. After a few minutes, they came to a gate where the road ended at a stone sheep pen. Then they were out upon the open hillside, climbing through wiry grass with a few stunted gorse bushes dotted like yellow beacons across the field.

Ahead of them, Awg was startled to see what he took to be a graveyard. This seemed a very odd place for such a thing – in so open a space, with no fence or hedge around and no church or other building nearby. As they drew closer, Awg saw that the objects he had taken to be rows of graves were in fact the whitened stumps of fallen trees. It was indeed a graveyard – the graveyard of an old forest, with the bleached skeletons of dead trees as tombstones.

After a gate in a wire fence, the path began to climb more obliquely, and soon the top of the mountain came into view. Awg and his grandmother reached the crest of the grassy ridge and began to walk along it to the summit. Below them, the increasingly steep slopes fell away in runs of scree and fields of boulders. Amidst them all, the mountain sheep picked their way sure-footedly along their precipitous tracks.

'Do they ever fall?' asked Awg.

'I suppose they must lose their footing sometimes,' said his grandmother, 'but I've never seen it. Their sense of balance is bred into them, I suppose. You ought to have a bit of it yourself, of course!'

'Whatever do you mean?' said Awg.

'Has your mother never said anything about Flossie?'

'No. I've never heard of her.'

'I'm not surprised. When we get home tonight, I'll look out something to show you.'

Nearing the summit of the mountain, the grassy path was becoming steep and rocky. At one point, it split up into a number of separate tracks, each leading off in a different direction. However, the way to the top was clear, because by the side of the main track a cross had been cut into the rock. The head of the cross was carved inside a circle, and the arms of the cross were joined by a delicate tracery of arcs and curves, their outline softened by centuries of weathering.

At the very top of the mountain was a large white boulder. At its apex, hikers had built a miniature cairn of stones, whilst to one side a flattened area made a natural seat.

'Eleven o'clock,' said his grandmother. 'Almost exactly the time that I arrived here with Joseph all those years ago – and we have followed exactly the same route on our way up.'

'So what happened when you got here?' asked Awg.

'Nothing, really. We climbed up on that rock and had our sandwiches.'

'We'll do the same,' said Awg, scrambling up. As he stood ready to help his grandmother on to the rock, he absent-mindedly reached over to the cairn of stones and slipped one of them into his pocket. Far above, two buzzards dipped and swirled.

Awg and his grandmother sat together in the stillness. The four valleys stretched out around them, rolling on and on until dissolving in the haze of higher mountains in the far distance. Beneath their feet, the open hillsides stood empty except for a scattering of sheep. Folded across the rougher pastures were the dark, forested slopes. Way below, the tiny stone-walled fields lay silent in a gentle patchwork of pastel colours.

Awg looked at his watch. The time was 11.14. Nearly the moment when his grandfather had vanished, ten years ago.

'Where were you, gran, and where was grandpa Joseph?' he asked, urgently.

'Grandpa Joseph was sitting on the rock, in the exact spot where you are now. I had climbed down on to the grass.'

She went to stand at the same place.

'He just looked down at the rock – down to his side and slightly to the right.'

Awg looked at his watch. The time was almost 11.15. The moment when his grandfather had disappeared. And he was sitting in the exact same spot.

Awg sat upon the rock.

His watch ticked away the last few moments.

He looked down. A ray of morning sunshine fell upon the white stone.

And Awg saw what his grandfather had seen a fraction of a second before he vanished.

Fifteen

It was just by his side, where a bit of the rock was smoother than the rest.

There was a mark on the rock, very small. Too small to have been carved. It was more like it had been pressed into the rock, like a seal in a piece of wax.

A strange symbol, a bit like a child's drawing of the sun.

The air was very still. Everything was quiet.

What should he say? Should he say anything? Awg didn't know what to do.

His grandmother broke the silence.

'Do you know, I have the strangest feeling that we're being watched.

'People say the early monks used to gather on Gellyn mountain to hold vigil at night. It's incredible to think that they were first here nearly a thousand years ago. They climbed the hill the same way we did, walked the same paths, stood in the same spot. I think they left their imprint on the landscape, that in a way they're here still.'

She went on, and Awg didn't know whether she was speaking to him, or simply voicing her thoughts out loud.

'I think that we're like fish in a pool – or perhaps more like bacteria under the microscope – unconscious of the observer. We're being watched by the monks – or perhaps by someone else.'

Awg wondered if his grandmother had her vanished husband in mind, but didn't dare ask. They walked home in sombre mood.

As they neared the house, it began to spot with rain and then to rain more heavily. They hurried inside, wet but not soaked.

Awg went upstairs to dry off and put on some warmer clothes. When he returned to the kitchen, he found tea ready and his grandmother smiling at a yellowed paper she had spread out on the table. It was a circus poster from the 1930s. There was nothing in it that looked familiar.

His grandmother laughed at his puzzled expression.

'I thought you might find it interesting,' she said, 'or do you know nothing at all about your mother's side of the family?'

'I know they're a very snooty lot,' said Awg. 'Her father was equerry to the Duke of Redbridge. Does that mean he looked after his horse?'

'No, I think it just means he was a Royal servant. Anyway, they weren't always so posh. *His* mother was Flossie the Human Fly.'

'No! You are *kidding*.'

'Absolutely not. They'd been a circus family for generations. Look at the poster. They called themselves The Three Tops: Flossie, her husband and her brother. It was a high wire act.

'I'm afraid she came to a bad end, though. Apparently she was a little too fond of the bottle.'

'Oh no! Did she get tipsy and fall?'

'No, it seems she did her act faultlessly – but then, when it was time to go off, she mistook the lion tunnel for the exit – and of course they're not fed until after the performance. All they ever found of her was one of her shoes.'

'Ugghh!'

Sixteen

Awg was getting ready for his Big Project.

As soon as he'd seen the hieroglyph on the boulder he knew it was identical to the one on the clock. That was why his grandfather had said "Well I never".

And then something had happened. Something so amazing and so powerful that he had been swallowed up in it and sucked out of the world.

The nature of that something was impossible to guess, but there was a clue – only a single clue, but it was a massive one.

He was going to put his idea into action that Thursday, as soon as his gran was safely on the bus to Pontrhyd for her weekly visit to the market. He didn't feel very happy about doing things on the sly, but he couldn't risk being forbidden to carry out his plan.

Awg had done his preparation carefully. He had read all the bits in his grandfather's books that dealt with eighteenth century clocks. There were also four other clocks in his grandfather's collection from around that time and he had examined them all closely. He was certain that he would find something unusual inside the black triangular clock and he wanted to make absolutely sure that he spotted it.

When Thursday morning at last arrived, Awg was in a fever of excitement. At breakfast, he knocked over the marmalade pot and found his hand shaking as he cleared it up. His grandmother looked questioningly at him but said nothing. She wondered if he was feeling unwell. He didn't have spots or look pale, so she decided that there could not be much the matter. She gathered her shopping things together and went off to catch the bus.

Awg took a deep breath. It was time to begin.

He had managed to find two stepladders, and one of them opened out to give a flat platform on the top. He positioned them both against the wall where the clock sat on its shelf. For a moment he hesitated. He knew it was a very valuable clock. What if something went badly wrong with his plan? Then he remembered the look in his grandmother's eyes when she was talking about grandpa.

Climbing up one set of steps, he edged the clock forward until he was able to get a firm grip on it and swing it down to the platform on the other stepladder.

Awg wedged the doors of the room and of his bedroom open and spread an old blanket over his grandfather's workbench. He then lifted the clock down and, holding it tightly against his chest, carried it slowly up the winding stair. With the clock safely on the bench, Awg was at last able to take a really good look at it.

Shock No. 1. The sides and back of the clock were perfectly smooth and plain. There was no little door for inspecting the works and no panel at the back to take off so that you could get to the mechanism inside. He tilted the clock backwards on its base. There was no way in from underneath, either. He looked at the face. It didn't open and the glass was sealed into the brass frame.

He turned the clock round so that the light shone fully on the back, and examined the surface with the magnifying glass. The only thing he could find was a tiny hole. At first he thought it might be a woodworm hole – not unusual in a wooden clock of that age! But it was too small and it looked too perfect. It had been made on purpose. Then he found a second hole, directly opposite the first. A crazy idea came into his head.

He ran downstairs and got two pins out of his gran's sewing box. He pushed one into each of the holes, finding that they went in about half an inch. He then took a pencil, braced it between the two pins and twisted it as if he were turning the dial on a radio. To his astonishment, it rotated quite easily, unscrewing like the lid of a jar. After a few turns, a circular ridge about six inches across stood up clear of the clock case. It took twelve more turns before a disc-like plug of wood came away, leaving a hole as big as his hand. The thread around the edge was extremely fine and Awg could see that it formed an almost perfect seal. No dirt or dust would get inside this clock.

But something had got inside. A piece of paper. There was a date and a signature: 'Joseph Bradley, Llangarreg'. So that was when his grandfather had worked on the clock. Here, on this very bench, fifteen years ago.

With the back removed, the voice of the clock could be heard more clearly: click ... uhh ... click ... uhh ... click ... uhh ... click ... . A gentle voice, soothingly calm.

Awg looked inside.

Shock No. 2. He had expected that the mechanism would be very complex, something especially intricate that had somehow kept the clock running for all those years.

It wasn't. It was very, very simple: five wheels, the basis of all clock movements.

The only remarkable thing about the movement as a whole was that it was made more like a watch than a clock, with beautifully jewelled bearings. Awg knew that these would give a long working life. But how long? And what kept the clock going?

The largest wheel in a clock is known as the great wheel. It is the driving wheel and is normally powered by a mainspring or by the action of a hanging weight. The mainspring is usually visible, or may be concealed inside a metal barrel.

In this clock, there was no mainspring. Sealed on to the great wheel was a small, flat cylinder of dull grey metal. On the side of the cylinder was a mark. Awg had been expecting to find it: a strange symbol, a bit like a child's drawing of the sun.

This was what had powered the clock for over two hundred years – and Awg was itching to find out what was inside it.

There was no way in.

The only sign that it was not completely solid was a faint line running all the way around the outside edge. Perhaps this was how you opened it.

Awg took the finest screwdriver from the rack and pressed it against the line, trying to force open a small crack.

Immediately, the note of the clock changed: clack … uurrhhh … clack … uurrhhh … clack … uurrhhh … clack …

The note became insistent and had a harsh edge to it.

Awg pressed a little harder. There was a loud humming noise.

For the first time, Awg had an uncomfortable feeling that what he was doing might be dangerous.

Awg pressed a little harder and twisted the screwdriver.

Someone shone a blinding light into his eyes.

Someone else grabbed him by the feet and whirled him round and round.

Someone else hit him over the head with a blunt, heavy object.

At least, that's what it felt like.

But there was no one else in the room.

Shock No. 3.

Seventeen

Awg opened his eyes. He did not feel good.

His mouth was completely dry and there was a piece of leather where his tongue used to be. He had a headache like the end of the world. His body felt as if it had been used for a trampoline by a family of hippos.

He was lying on his back. The bed, without sheets or blankets, was made of a dark, rubbery material. There was a dim light from a window high up in the wall. The room was very small.

Awg rolled over and tried to sit up. Something sharp jabbed into his side. He found he was still holding the screwdriver. In fact, he was more than holding it. His hand was locked on it with his fingers clasped round the handle in a vice-like grip. The fingers were cold and he couldn't feel them.

With his other hand, he prised the fingers open and slipped the screwdriver into his top pocket. Then he rubbed the fingers and tried to work them. Gradually, the numbness wore off and the feeling crept back. At last, he found that he could begin to move them again.

He was dressed in his jeans and tee shirt and he still had his hoodie jacket on. It had been cold in his bedroom. But this wasn't his bedroom. There was no sign of the clock, of the circular workroom, of the castle, of anything that he was familiar with.

He swung his legs down and sat on the edge of the bed. There was a small table, made of the same rubbery stuff. Apart from that, there was nothing in the room. Absolutely nothing. Four grey walls, a window and a door.

Gingerly, he stood up, and found his legs very wobbly. He began to stumble slowly around the room. After a few minutes, he felt better and the stumble became a walk. Four paces up, two paces across, four paces up, two paces across.

He looked up at the window. It was high, but not impossibly high. He put the table on the bed and climbed up on it. Standing right up, he was still well below the window but at least he could get some sort of view through it. He had to find out where he was.

It was night-time, and the sky looked very odd. There were so many stars. It was ablaze with light. He tried to find something he recognised. There was no Plough, no Great Bear.

Perhaps he was in Australia. Then you'd get the Southern Cross instead of the Pole Star. And Orion would be the wrong way up, with his sword pointing upwards.

No Southern Cross. No Orion.

But there were two large moons – and one of them was green.

Eighteen

Awg was glad about the two moons, especially the green one. It gave him a fairly good clue that he was almost certainly no longer in Wales.

Q. Where can you go and see a blazingly bright sky with no stars you recognise and two moons, one of them green?

A. (1) Nowhere you can get to on a bus

(2) Nowhere on the surface of the Earth

(3) Nowhere inside the Earth, unless Jules Verne was right and all the geologists are wrong

(4) Nowhere in your right mind.

So that leaves: either you're a long way from the Earth, or you're out of your skull.

If you're out of your skull, how do you *know* you are? Your fantasy world might be so realistic you'd never know until you woke up, or came round, or whatever.

Perhaps that small, grey cylinder in the clock had released a mind-altering drug and the only trip he was on was inside his head.

Awg forced his eyes open very wide and clenched his fists until the fingernails dug in and hurt. Then he opened his hands and inspected the white marks on the palms. He decided that the feel of everything around him was enough to convince him of reality – and if it *was* all chemicals then he'd just have to wait and see if they wore off.

He craned his neck round in every possible direction. The only result of this was that the table wobbled alarmingly and he nearly fell off it. But no, he couldn't see anything else through the window except that very remarkable sky. No side views of another part of the building he was in. And no sign of any other building. Or anything that might give a hint as to where the ground might be.

This must mean either (a) he wasn't in a building at all but somewhere else entirely – like a spacecraft, or (b) he was in a tall, isolated building, like a tower.

If he was in a spacecraft it had to be a mighty big one, with some system of artificial gravity. You don't nearly fall off tables in a weightless environment. And a spaceship with rooms like this had to be really boring. Awg expected spaceships to be excitingly bright and shiny with lots of mind-blowing gadgets and stuff. The tower option seemed much more likely, although disappointing – and possibly more life threatening.

A very small room in a tower. A room he couldn't get out of. Perhaps he could start with doing something about that.

Four grey walls, a window and a door. He tried digging at the walls with his screwdriver. Hopeless. It didn't leave so much as a mark on them. And he couldn't reach the window.

That left the door. You could tell it was a door because there was a thin rectangular outline in the wall the size and shape of a door. But any handle or lock must be on the outside because there was no sign of them. And he was on the inside. Awg tried the screwdriver in the door-shaped crack. The gap was so small you couldn't even get the tip of the blade inside.

A very small room in a tower. A tower on somewhere that wasn't the Earth. Well, at least that was a start. All he had to do now was find out where he was, how he had got here, and how he could get home again.

Awg had an uncomfortable feeling that none of these was going to be all that easy. Perhaps it would help if he screamed and ran around in circles waving his arms.

No, it just meant that he had an awful lot to learn.

And it meant that, if the door of the room opened and an eight foot tall alien covered in metallic scales and bristling with fearsome weaponry came in, he should be prepared for it.

Nineteen

The door hadn't opened yet but it was going to. Somebody, or something, was outside. Awg jumped down and slammed the table back in its place. He sat on the bed and waited.

A small panel in the door was pulled back and a face appeared. It was not a welcoming face. And it did not belong to his grandmother.

The panel was slid shut with a crash and there was the sound of the door being unlocked. The owner of the face came into the room. The body attached to the face was roughly human in shape and was not covered in scales.

'Jqwvdjc bgmnmb cjkqwxds qjyghdlonm ljhdc,' said the owner of the face.

A tray was held out towards him with two pills on it. They were about the size of aspirin tablets but were bright blue and full of tiny holes like a piece of pumice.

Awg wondered if the pills were something for his headache. They were going to be difficult to swallow without a glass of water. In any case, he was certainly not going to take anything without a good idea of what it was first.

'What are they?' Awg asked.

'Vawd lkjwemnmsacni khds!!!'

That sounded like an order. Awg did nothing.

The owner of the face grabbed him roughly by the arm and stuck one of the pills in his left ear, then stepped back and pointed at the other pill.

Awg stuck the second pill in his right ear.

'About bloody time! I thought I was never gonna get you sorted.'

'Where am I?' asked Awg.

'Prison, o'course. Where else d'you think?'

'But – why?'

'Come off it! You Outlanders is all the same. Very happy to use the technology but don't want to stick to the bleedin' rules.'

'How long am I going to be here?'

'This is just Recov'ry. Now you've woke up you'll be moved, prob'ly tomorra'. Then you'll start to do your time proper.'

He pulled a shiny, rectangular object out of his tunic. It was about the size and shape of an exercise book but seemed to be made of black glass.

'Let's see. Abuse of a RS21 power unit: 5 years 3 months and eleven days.'

The owner of the face ran a finger along rows and columns of hieroglyph-like symbols. Not a hand, just a finger.

'Any previous convictions?'

'Uh ... N-No,' stammered Awg, baffled what he should say.

'First offence.' The finger moved along a row. 'Appendix 42.'

Screenpages of symbols flicked rapidly by.

'Ah, 'ere we are. Abuse of RS21 power unit, first offence: 5 years 3 months and ten days. There's leniency for you.'

The owner of the face stared at Awg. The eye showed obvious interest, although the face itself was expressionless.

'Where you from? 46598264 more'n likely. They're always muckin' us about. Am I right?'

'I'm from Strenton. At least, I was. Then I was at Llangarreg.'

'Never heard of either of 'em. What sector they in?'

'Sector?'

'I bet you're gonna say where you lives they still uses the old addresses with the planet names in. We're up to date here. Sector, coordinates – that's it. Much quicker.'

He stuffed the noteglass back inside his tunic, then looked down again at Awg.

'Actually, we scanned yer head for yer tag but it didn't show up. That's an offence, too – everyone here's supposed to be tagged. But they found they couldn't apply it to visitors.'

'Visitors? You said this was a prison!'

'Yeah, that's right. But you don't live here so you got to be a visitor, ain't you?'

The logic of this seemed undeniable.

'So, if I'm a visitor I don't need a tag?' said Awg.

'No, the law got thrown out. Discrimination, o'course.'

'Discrimination?'

'The rule said you got to have an identity tag in yer head. Simple process – they just bore a hole in yer head and stick it in.'

Awg was suddenly grateful he was a visitor.

'But it didn't suit the Nerians,' continued his captor.

'They thought it was a bad idea to have a hole bored in your head?'

'Nah, nah – wasn't like that at all. The problem was, *Nerians* don't actually *have* a head, as such – and the law definitely said *in the head* – so it was ruled to be cranial discrimination and got chucked out.'

The owner of the face turned towards the door.

'Well, nice talkin' to you. Want anythin', by the way?'

'I'd like something to eat – and drink,' said Awg, without much hope of success.

'Food? I'm not sure visitors is allowed food. I'll go an' look it up.'

The owner of the face trudged out, locking the door behind him.

Seems a cheerful enough sort, thought Awg. After all, being a jailer can't be a very fulfilling job.

Anyway, it was probably unwise to argue with a guard whose skin was a uniform, metallic grey and who in other respects appeared to be an eight foot tall heavily-armed alien.

Twenty

This couldn't be happening. You don't stick a screwdriver into a clock in Wales and then wake up to find yourself in prison on a different planet. It's impossible.

On the other hand, clocks don't usually run for two hundred years and it isn't exactly normal for monks and grandfathers to suddenly vanish into thin air. Awg felt that his definition of impossible was in urgent need of revision.

He glanced around his cell: four grey walls, a window and a door. It looked exactly the same as it had done when he first woke up. Awg knew with horrible certainty that he wasn't dreaming. He wasn't out of his skull. This was Reality. And if it wasn't the reality he was used to he'd better come to terms with it, because it didn't look as if the old one was coming back any time soon.

Four grey walls, a window and a door – or rather, a suggestion of where a door might be. Awg stared again at the rectangular outline in the wall. It seemed to him that its edge was fuzzier, blacker than before. But something didn't feel quite right.

Suddenly, a surge of hope. Perhaps the door wasn't really shut. Perhaps the jailor hadn't locked it properly. Awg had only to press against it and it would swing open. There would be an empty corridor. He would run down it and find his way out. He would be free. Yes!

But his jailor didn't look the type who made mistakes. If the door *was* unlocked, it was unlocked for a reason. Perhaps there was no real intention to keep him as a prisoner. Prisoners were an encumbrance. They took up space and had to be looked after, given food and water. Far better to get rid of them.

Awg ran the scene again. He would press against the door and it would swing open. There would be an empty corridor. He would run down it – and a bolt of energy would rearrange the molecules in his body so that they were splattered around the walls and not a great deal of use to him any more. *Shot trying to escape* – the oldest trick in the book.

But at least he ought to test out the first step.

Awg got up and took the two paces across the width of his cell. He confronted the dark line traced in the wall. He placed his hands against it. Paused. Then pushed hard.

There was not the slightest hint of movement. Torn between disappointment and relief, Awg staggered back to the bed and slumped down.

The something that hadn't felt quite right now felt it worse. And there was a drumming noise in his ears.

Awg lay there waiting for something to happen.

He waited a long time.

Nothing did.

The door did not open again. The jailor did not reappear and Awg became increasingly conscious of hunger and thirst. Perhaps the warder would never return and he would just be left to die. He listened for the sounds of other prisoners, or any sounds at all. He could hear nothing except the sick-making beat of the drumming in his ears. Bright pinpoints of light began to float in front of his eyes.

*

For the many higher life forms in the Universe, plasma transport is a hazardous business. The physiological effects of passage through a matter transfer beam are unpredictable; especially on the first occasion, and particularly if proper preparation has not been made beforehand. Unknown to himself, Awg was showing the first signs of *pericellular necrosis*, in which critical body functions slow down and eventually stop. This is widely considered to be a bad idea.

The condition is caused by damage to the various enzyme systems of the body and can be quickly reversed by a simple rehydration procedure. Without help, it leads first to disturbances of vision, then to increasing periods of ever deeper sleep, and finally to death.

Awg's jailor had no intention of leaving him to perish. On purpose, that is – with malice aforethought. He was in fact a relatively kindly being whose main concern was to do his work methodically and keep himself secure in a good, steady job. At the present moment he was showing his concern for Awg's welfare by wading through the oceans of rules and regulations describing in detail the separate ways in which the one hundred and seventy-three different categories of prisoner should be treated.

It would be many hours before he came to the section in the Penitentiary Operative's Manual which told him to analyse the body type of the prisoner and take remedial action for any harm suffered in the plasma transport process. It is merely unfortunate that the entire backroom investigation is likely to take him several days, by which time any way in which Awg might have been treated will be of theoretical interest only.

*

Awg lay on the bed. He had no idea that the cells in his body were starting to look around for the *off* switch. What he was mostly thinking about was the length of his sentence and how he could cope with it. But he was not thinking too clearly.

His throat was parched with thirst, and his headache had settled into a dull throbbing pain like Black Sabbath on really bad headphones. He began drifting into sleep. Certain words kept going through his head. They were *five years three months and ten days.*

Twenty One

There was a noise at the window. Awg woke up.

There was a sawing noise, and it was definitely at the window. Then there was a *zzzzuuckkkk* as powerful sucker pads were attached to the outside, and suddenly the window was no longer there.

A rope spiralled down to the floor and a figure slid into the room.

Awg did a quick check. Face: almost human. Eyes: more than one and less than three. Weapons: none visible. He was learning.

'Get up that rope, quick!'

'But who ...'

'Shurrup. Get up the rope!'

Awg tried to stand but found that his legs seemed to have turned to rubber. He slid to the floor.

The girl stuck her hand in front of his face.

'Colour?'

'Eh?'

'What colour's my hand?'

'It's a bit blurred ... but sort of yellow, I think. Or maybe it's red.'

'Thought so. Drink this.'

The girl produced a black tube and snapped open a cap on the end.

'Water and mineral salts,' she said. 'Drink it very slowly. Not a moment too soon, by the look of you.'

Awg took a swig, and choked.

'I said *slowly*. You're dehydrated, and your body's gone into shock after your transfer. It happens sometimes.'

Awg drank. It had a slightly bitter, salty taste but it was like the sweetest spring water to his parched throat.

'Now wait.'

After a few minutes, she held out her hand again.

'Now?'

'Brownish-white. Definitely.'

'That's better. Can you get up?'

Awg found to his surprise that he could stand quite easily. He walked around the room.

'Recovery's usually pretty quick,' said the girl. 'You'll be fine. Now get up that rope!'

Awg grasped the rope, locked it between his knees and feet and shinned up towards the window. He had to stop a couple of times to take a few deep breaths, but then he was away to the top.

'Good,' she said. 'Climb through and wait on the ledge.'

The ledge was narrow. Awg squatted at one end, hanging on to the edges of the hole where the window had been. He was beginning to feel almost normal again – or at least as normal as you can feel clinging to a prison window ledge on an unknown planet.

A head appeared at Awg's level. It had two eyes and was attached to the girl. She pulled up the rope and flicked it down the outside of the building.

'Go down, and wait at the bottom. Lie flat.'

Awg did as he was told. The girl climbed out, took the window off the hooks she had stapled into the wall, sprayed a brown gel around the edges and slotted it back into its hole. In a moment she was down beside Awg.

'Covering our tracks. With a bit of luck they'll think you faded again. Happens occasionally when the plasma's unstable. You can sit up now.'

Awg found that they were on the roof of a vast, square building, sitting beneath the walls of a tower which rose several stories above its centre.

'You came into the plasma chamber at the top,' said the girl, pointing upwards. 'The rest of the tower's where the recovery rooms are. The survivors get moved into cells in the main block.'

'Survivors?'

'Mortality rate's about five percent for unmoderated plasma transfer, so a few don't make it. Quite dodgy really.'

Awg suddenly felt sick. 'But ...'

'No time now. Got to get over the edge.'

Away from the central tower, the roof of the huge building was completely flat until you reached the edge, where there was a raised parapet some three feet high.

The girl took out a transparent rod about the size of a pencil. She crawled forward a few yards and held it up. After a few seconds it glowed with a faint blue light, then faded, then shone out again. She waited until this had happened several times and then crawled back to Awg.

'Beam detector,' said the girl. 'Two pulses seven seconds apart, repeated after one minute. They change the frequency every half-hour, so you've always got to check.

'That means we've got a minute to get across to the edge. Run when I say and lie flat against the wall.'

She took up her former position and fixed her eyes on the rod.

'Now!'

Awg shot across the open space and crashed down by the wall. Another minute, and the girl was beside him again.

'What would have happened if the beams had hit us?' asked Awg.

'With the first one, nothing – that's just detection. As soon as it finds something, the energy in the second beam goes sky high. It'll burn through armoured plate. People just leave a black stain.'

The girl leant over the parapet. There were two gunshots. Awg threw himself flat on the ground.

'Sorry,' said the girl. 'Should have warned you. Just fixing the anchor. Now – put this on.'

Awg slipped his legs and arms through the harness, then fastened the clasp at his waist.

The girl helped him over the top of the parapet. Awg expected to find a rope or a wire ladder. There was neither.

'Lower yourself until you feel the line tighten,' she said. 'Then use the control on the right side of your belt. The more you press, the faster it reels out.'

Awg felt hesitantly around the belt. He was still thinking about the second beam – and trying to stop himself shaking.

'What's ... what's the button on the left side for?' he whispered.

'It releases the line – so it's not a good idea to press it on the way down. Do that when you've reached the bottom so I can follow you.'

Awg clutched the top of the parapet, his elbows bent and his body hunched up. Across the expanse of roof, the tower reared above him, a black silhouette against the brilliantly starlit sky. He glanced down and wished he hadn't. The wall was shear and its base was in shadow, but the drop looked at least a hundred feet.

He began to relax his arms, dropping slowly into emptiness and seemingly without anything above that might keep him from falling. As his arms reached nearly their full stretch, he felt the harness tightening around him. He let go of the parapet and found himself swinging in space, supported as if by nothing. He reached up and touched the invisible thread that was stopping him plunging to the unseen ground. He could feel it, thin as a strand of spider silk and as hard and taut as a bowstring under his weight.

Awg pressed on the button at his waist and gasped as he shot downwards, much too fast, bumping and scraping against the rough wall. He came to a stop and steadied himself against the side of the stonework. He pressed again, much more gently. Soon, he found he could control his rate of descent, arching his body away from the wall and using his feet to keep himself clear. Suddenly he hit the ground, and his legs buckled under the shock.

He checked to make sure he was really on the ground and not on a ledge, then pressed the stud on the left of his belt. He felt a jerk as the line detached. A few minutes later, the girl was at his side.

'Now listen,' she said. 'This is the dangerous bit.'

Awg gulped.

Twenty Two

Awg stole a glance at what lay ahead. It was an utterly barren landscape. Grey sand and scattered rocks stretched in all directions. There were no bushes or trees, but here and there he could see small patches of a spiky, reddish lichen. A thought struck him and he checked around the sky. The second moon was still green, so he hadn't imagined it.

The girl produced another of the black tubes and snapped open the cap.

'Just water this time,' she said. 'but remember to drink it slowly.'

Awg sipped the water carefully. He had a feeling it would have to last him for quite a while.

The girl was dressed in a loose grey tunic. She was looking at his grey hoodie and dark blue jeans.

'Your clothes are good for the desert,' she said. 'Effective camouflage.'

'How long before they'll come looking?' asked Awg.

'Possibly never, but we can't take that chance.' She opened a water tube for herself and drank.

'We've got to get across about five miles of desert before dawn. When it gets light we're more easily spotted and then there's the heat as well.'

She took a compass-like instrument from her pocket and aligned two of the three needles with the horizon.

They walked quickly across the rough terrain. After about a quarter of a mile, they came to a fence. It was made of a dense wire mesh but was only about two feet high.

'Perimeter fence,' said the girl. 'It makes a complete ring around the prison. Careful – it's electrified.'

She stepped cautiously over and Awg followed. He was puzzled to see that the outside of the fence was covered in scorch marks and tufts of coarse grey fur.

The girl made for the far side of a group of rocks. She sat down and pulled Awg down beside her.

'We're out of sight here, but it's extremely dangerous. We've got to get the protection on.'

Awg gazed around, feeling rather foolish. There was nothing to be seen except rocks and grey sand. The girl, who was watching the ground around them intently, darted a glance at him.

'Remember the fence?' she asked.

'Yes, of course. But it isn't going to keep anything in, is it? Anyone escaping from the prison would hardly notice it.' Unless they were midgets, he thought, and small midgets at that.

'Anyone with any sense would stay *inside* the fence rather than outside. That way at least there would be a fair chance of staying alive. It's not made for keeping things in. It's for keeping things out. That fence is only two feet high but it goes down another twenty feet into the ground. It's there to protect the prison from the balerids.'

'Balerids?'

'Flesh-eating desert rats. They're absolutely lethal. It's impossible to cross the desert if you're unprepared. Nothing can survive out here where the balerids are.'

'How big are they, then?' asked Awg, who had visions of rats the size of wolves.

'Oh, they're tiny – about the size of your thumb.'

'Are you winding me up?' said Awg indignantly. 'If so, it's not very funny.'

The girl glared at him.

'Their teeth make up forty percent of their body weight, and most of the rest's jaw muscle. It's estimated that at any point in the desert there are about fifty within a ten foot radius. They can scent blood up to a mile away and then up to a hundred thousand will swarm in. A half-ton animal can be reduced to its skeleton in under five minutes. *Satisfied?* Now, *get going*.'

She produced a small jar.

'Cover your arms and legs in it – and you'd better put a bit on your face and neck as well, to be sure.'

Awg opened the jar. It was full of a foul smelling brown slime. He stuck his finger in and rubbed an experimental smear on his arm. He raised it to his nose and sniffed – then retched at the stench.

'Uggghhh! It's *disgusting*. What is it?'

'Don't ask.'

'But what's it for?'

'It's to prevent the first bite. It's OK as long as they don't scent blood.'

Awg scanned the ground in alarm and quickly put the ointment on. The smell wafted around him and his stomach churned.

They trudged across the wasteland. It was bitterly cold but Awg suspected things might get worse when the sun – or possibly suns – came up. Behind them, the brilliant starlight was beginning to be overtaken by a brighter haze and he sensed that dawn was approaching.

'You said we had to go about five miles – how far is it now?' Awg asked.

The girl pointed at a darker line in the lightening greyness ahead. 'We're heading west – towards those hills. There's an old fort built into the hillside and there are caves behind. It used to be the prison before Tukzadryk was built but it's been deserted for years. You'll meet some of my friends there. We use it as one of our bases.'

'Who are you?' said Awg. 'And why are helping me like this? You don't know who I am or anything about me.'

'It's not important who I am – and I don't need to know who you are, or where you're from. I'm doing it to save you rotting in jail. There are so few prisoners now and they just get forgotten.

At one time there were thousands. It's an archaic system. No one deserves to rot in Tukzadryk.'

They laboured on. As the heat intensified, their progress slowed, but gradually the dark line became a range of low hills and they found themselves on rising ground. The terrain changed. Previously, it had been coarse sand and large rocks. Now the sand took on the consistency of dust and their feet kicked up choking grey clouds of it. The stacks of rocks gave way to outcrops of small, sharp stones.

Once over the smooth crest of the rise, they could see the old fort, its sinister square outline breaking the monotony of the hillside below them. The girl's pace began to quicken and Awg found his feet slipping and skidding on the treacherous ground in his efforts to keep up.

Suddenly, he lost his footing and fell, sliding and rolling down the slope. He dug his heels in and glissaded to a halt amidst a shower of razor-edged flints. Knowing he was hurt, he called out, but the girl was now too far ahead to hear. Awg got shakily to his feet and stumbled after her. Pain pulsed in his leg and a dark red patch was spreading from the rip in his jeans.

He had gone only a few paces when he felt a new sensation in his leg: something sharp and penetrating. An attack. A bite. It forced him to a standstill. He pulled up his jeans and saw a small grey shape locked on to his calf. It clung there, its powerful teeth sinking into his flesh. Awg stood transfixed, as if he were watching a picture on a screen. Even the pain seemed to be at a distance. As he watched, another of the tiny rats climbed on to his leg. And then two more, licking at the blood. And then five more. Awg shook his leg and kicked furiously, but it had no effect whatever. The rats clung on like magnets. He felt something on his back and a rat ran down his arm. He tried to flick it off but it ran up his neck and got tangled in his hair, wriggling and scrabbling. He looked down and saw a writhing mass of grey swarming around his feet.

The rat on his head broke free, tearing out tufts of his black hair by the roots and crawling down on to his face.

Awg panicked. The girl heard his cries and ran back.

'Shut your eyes!' she screamed.

Awg heard the roar of the burner. A wave of heat engulfed him – and then he was choking with the acrid stench of burning fur. Awg felt the rats drop off one by one. In the darkness of his tight-shut eyes, charring flesh hissed and crackled. Then the girl grasped his hand and they were stumbling, falling, running, running, running down the hill.

A metal door crashed shut and they collapsed together on the floor.

Twenty Three

The girl helped Awg to his feet. They left the metal entrance door behind them and climbed several floors to the highest level at the front of the building. The room Awg found himself in was slightly less filthy and derelict than the others they had passed, and contained a table and metal bunks by the inner wall. The outer wall was only half the height of the room so that the upper part was open to the air. There were the remains of metal fixings at regular intervals along the top and deep bolt holes had been drilled down into the stonework.

'This was one of the lookout bunkers,' said the girl. 'All the old kit's been stripped out, so it's safe to use. And no one can approach without being observed. You can see for miles across the desert.'

Awg sank down on one of the metal bunks. He pulled off his jacket. There were scorch marks all down one side.

'Are you burned?' asked the girl.

'Not much,' replied Awg, weakly. 'But my hair's a bit singed, judging by the smell.' He stretched himself out on the bunk and tried to relax.

'It's my fault,' she said. 'I shouldn't have gone so far ahead and left you. You can rest now. We're safe here.'

After a while, Awg began to feel a bit less shattered. The girl cleaned up the gash on his leg and covered it with a strip of a yellow parchment-like substance.

'It protects the wound,' she said, 'and then peels off when the skin is healed.'

She inspected his damaged limb with interest.

'You've got fur on your leg, like an animal,' she said. 'That's freaky! Do you have fur all over?'

'It's not fur, it's hair,' said Awg. 'Most people have it on their heads. But it can grow in other places as well.'

'Can you grow it wherever you like?'

'How d'you mean?'

'Well, if you worked in a cold place, could you grow more on your arms and legs to help you keep warm?'

'No, it doesn't work like that. It just grows where it wants to. You can't control it.'

'What if it suddenly grew all over your face so you couldn't see where you were going?'

'It doesn't work like that either – and it only grows slowly, anyway.'

The girl grinned and pulled down the leg of Awg's jeans.

'You should have really yelled out as soon as you got hurt. I was too keen to check if the others had arrived. I'm sorry. You must have been terrified – the balerids are vile.'

Awg turned on to his side and got his leg as comfortable as he could.

'It was mainly the numbers that scared me. I didn't think so many could come so quickly. It was only the first rat that actually bit me. I suppose the bleeding had washed off some of the ointment. The rest of them were frightened of the stuff – I could tell. That's what really shook me – it was seriously weird.'

'Why was that?'

'I could understand the noises they made – what they were saying! At first it was 'Food, Food!', then when they smelt the ointment it was 'Danger, Danger!'. Then when you got out that flame thrower it was 'Run, Run!'

'That's because of the translocution modules in your ears. They're very sophisticated. They pick up all types of communication signals between animals: not just speech sounds but brain waves too. They even use the nerve transmissions from your own eyes to gather more information. What you hear is a complete synthesis of all the communication feedback

– converted to sound impulses you can understand. If you transferred the modules to another person, they would adapt to the new wearer.'

'You mean if I was listening to something, and then I gave the modules to someone else, they would understand the same thing but the actual sounds they heard would be different.'

'Exactly.'

'It was scary. I didn't expect to hear rats talking. Especially ones that looked at me as their next meal.'

He remembered something that had puzzled him.

'One thing about the balerids – you said there were millions of them in the desert. But it's a desert – there's nothing there. What do they live on?'

'The desert grows every year. There used to be other small animals but few are left now. There were many plants, even trees. Now there are only the patches of brown desert grass. The balerids eat that when they can get nothing else. But mostly it's worse. They eat each other.'

Awg shuddered.

'And what about the ointment,' he asked. 'What is it?'

'I told you – you really *don't* want to know.'

The girl gave him a grim smile. He was obviously going to persist.

'The balerids are afraid of only one thing. They have a natural predator. There's a parasitic worm that burrows into their skin and kills them. They know it by its smell and are instinctively afraid of it. So if you breed the worms ...

'And then boil them up to kill them and destroy any dangerous bacteria they might be carrying ...

'And then mash them into a pulp ...

'You get a sort of brown slime ...'

Awg knew he shouldn't have asked.

Twenty Four

The old fort was vast. Awg soon discovered that the ugly stone building sticking out of the hill was only a tiny part of the huge complex of rooms, passageways and cells that made up the stronghold. Some of it incorporated natural caves; other parts had been quarried out of the hillside. Most of the structure was out of sight, going down level upon level into the rock.

'Impressive, isn't it?' said the girl. 'But this is only a fraction of the size of Tukzadryk. You can only guess at the size of that place, or how many prisoners are still there. We know that there are at least sixty levels below ground.'

Awg felt hugely relieved that he was no longer a prisoner himself. Five years three months and ten days was a large slice out of your life – especially when you didn't know what you'd done wrong or how you'd ended up where you were.

'What are you going to do when your friends get here?' he asked.

'Check if they're being followed, then find out what they've discovered.'

'Are they on the run from prison too?'

The girl laughed. 'Yes, I suppose they are. In a sense, we all are.'

'Even you?' said Awg in amazement.

'Especially me – the one who must *not* be caught!'

'But you said nobody would come looking for us. So does that mean we're safe now?'

'You are. We're not.'

They were sitting in the lookout room, sharing some food.

The girl had two sorts of basic rations: Awg was not wildly enthusiastic about either of them. There was a green biscuit that smelt of seaweed and stuck to your teeth as you tried to chew it. The girl said it was high in protein and very nutritious. Then there was a brown powder you mixed with water to make a gritty porridge that tasted of cardboard. Apparently that gave you your carbohydrates. Awg decided that food here was not meant to be enjoyed. He went back to his questioning.

'But I'm an escaped prisoner – why aren't they hunting for me? It doesn't make sense.'

'That's because you don't understand how the system works. It's entirely dependent on fixed rules and regulations. The prison staff have no responsibility for you outside Tukzadryk. If you escape, it's the job of the desert patrol to find you.'

'So what'll happen when they discover I'm not there any more?'

'Once they find you're not in your cell, this is what they'll do. First, they'll think you've faded, so they'll go through the plasma records. With a bit of luck, most of the documentation will be out of date or missing, so it'll take them ages. Then, they'll have to check out the procedure for reporting a lost prisoner. That'll probably take days as well.

'Even if they come round to the idea you might somehow have escaped, all the zwnerbas will do is alert the desert patrols to keep a look out for your bones. They think it's impossible to cross the desert because of the balerids. No one has ever escaped from Tukzadryk and lived.'

'Would a zwnerba be grey-skinned, one-eyed and about eight feet tall?' asked Awg.

'Yes, that's right. They're a big part of our community on Zero. They run everything. They're quite OK provided you stick to the rules. That's how everything's supposed to work – by the rules.'

'You said *Zero?*' said Awg. 'What's *Zero?*'

'Zero's where you are now. It's the planet with the oldest civilisation in the galaxy. It's called Zero because the numeric position of everywhere else is given in reference to it. So the coordinates of Zero itself are [00,00,00,00].'

Awg choked on a piece of the gluey biscuit. He swallowed hard and tried to get his mind properly tuned in to what the girl had said. So he was stuck on a planet called Zero, sitting in an abandoned prison with … someone – and eating … something. Awg chomped on the flavourless mush and had visions of the burger and chips at the café in Strenton where he hung out with his mates. And about the fabulous meals he'd had with his gran at Llangarreg. He wondered if he'd ever see either place again.

He forced his mind back to the present, and to the girl. As to what he was eating – well, he remembered the stuff about the balerid ointment. There were some things it was better not to know.

'So why am I safe and not you?' he said. 'Why are they after you – what did you all do?'

'We asked questions.'

'What's wrong in that? It's not a crime to ask questions.'

'Perhaps not, but it can be very unhealthy.'

'You mean, if people have something bad to hide?'

'Exactly,' said the girl.

'But *I* didn't ask any questions. I didn't do *anything* – and the next thing I knew I was in prison.'

'If you were in prison, you must have broken one of our laws.'

'I wasn't breaking any laws, I was mending a clock,' said Awg indignantly but not entirely truthfully.

'Well, something you did must have involved the misuse of our technology. Which planet did you come from – 56394762? or 46598264? What was its number, its coordinates?'

'I don't know. I don't think it had any.'

'Everywhere has a number. If you were using our technology, you must have come from a planet in our galaxy.'

'The jailer at Tukzadryk said something about an RS21 power unit. That must have been the thing I was trying to open.'

'There you are! It must have had an *inspection prohibited* clause in the licence. You committed an offence for which there was an automatic penalty – so you were auto-extradited to Tukzadryk for punishment. That's the way it all works. Law enforcement is linked directly into the plasma transport system.'

'You mean if people do something wrong, they're zonked straight into jail for it?'

'Yes, if that's the prescribed punishment. Any offence is immediately analysed and the penalty applied automatically.'

'But that's horrendous!'

'No, it's not. Not necessarily, anyway. It worked very well for many years. People stopped breaking the law because they *always* got caught. Places like Tukzadryk lay almost empty and we had a crime-free society. People of my father's generation are convinced that's still the case.'

'And isn't it?' asked Awg.

'No. Something's gone wrong. There's corruption everywhere and people's lives are getting ruined. Most of the victims have no way of fighting back, because it's impossible to tell which Officials are crooks and which ones are still honest. Ordinary people have no one they can trust. So a group of us are trying to do something about it.'

'And you're their leader?'

'Yes.'

There was a long silence.

Awg knew he had to ask.

'So what do you do – you and these friends of yours? Organise protests and blow up government buildings and kill people?'

The girl turned on him furiously, her eyes blazing.

'What would that achieve? And if that *was* our business, why would I waste my time on you? I would leave you to fester away in Tukzadryk or die in the desert.'

Seeing the effect of her outburst upon Awg, her tone softened.

'We have to change the system from within. Only if everyone accepts the need can any lasting reform be made. *Everyone*, from the lowest to the highest. Perhaps especially the highest ...'

She paused and seemed lost in thought, but then recovered herself.

'So we watch, we investigate, we collect the evidence. The group you'll meet here are working near the arterial road, about two miles away. They're carrying out surveillance on the desert convoys.'

'So are ... are these convoys transporting something valuable?' asked Awg, still shaken, and wishing that he had not put his earlier question so bluntly. 'Something that might get hijacked?'

'They carry many things between our cities, but my friends are interested only in one – a cargo which on this planet is rare and costly.'

'Like gold, or diamonds?'

'We have both in abundance and they're of comparatively little value, except as industrial materials. No, our focus is on the fleets of tankers. They travel under armed guard, but, even so, much of their contents never reaches its destination. It is stolen.'

'Oil?'

'You're probably still thinking in terms of your own planet. If you travelled around the galaxy, you'd discover that the needs and values of the different peoples vary enormously from place to place. On Zero, our most valuable commodity is water.'

Water! Awg had not been surprised at the absence of streams or pools as they crossed the desert, but it had not occurred to him that the scarcity might be far more widespread.

'But if someone's stealing the water,' he said, 'surely the thieves get found out and zoomed off into prison by your automatic system?'

'That's the theory. In reality, no activation of the auto-policing system takes place. The drivers report no incidents, and the seals on the tanks are unbroken when they arrive. Officially, the theft has never happened. But much of the water will have gone, and it will end up on the black market.'

'So how does the water get taken, and why doesn't the automatic system nab those who are doing it?'

'That's precisely what my friends and I are trying to find out. And of course there are many other scams besides the water. There's so much to investigate. Places like Tukzadryk are being used to get rid of people who won't do as they're told. That's why we take a special interest in new arrivals and try to get them out.'

'And you found me!'

'Most of those dumped into them now are like you – they haven't done much wrong. I've got a good friend whose son began to ask awkward questions at the food factory where he worked. Then the boss tricked him into breaking one of the minor Laws. He's in one of the prisons somewhere but we can't find him. We've been searching for over a year.'

For about the twentieth time that day, the girl went over to the bunker wall and looked out, scanning the empty desert and staring towards the horizon.

She turned back to Awg.

'You get some sleep and I'll keep watch. The others should arrive soon.'

Something in her voice made him look up.

'You worried?' he asked.

For the first time, the girl seemed momentarily less confident, her gaze less defiant.

'When our Group first started, we made no progress for a long time. Every line of investigation ended up against a blank wall. Eventually, we managed to hack into the zwnerba records system and were able to do some real checking. Not long after, we got the first indication we were beginning to get near the people behind all this.'

'How d'you know that?'

'They began trying to kill us.'

Twenty Five

When Awg awoke, the pain from the gash in his leg was almost gone. The parchment-like substance seemed to have fused with his skin so that it was difficult to see where the skin ended and the dressing began. All the angry redness around the wounds had dispersed, so the parchment must have contained a whole raft of disinfectant and healing components. Awg felt that a rat-bite out in the wilds of the desert might otherwise not be a very clever thing to have.

The girl was using some form of communication device and was obviously not getting the results she wanted. Awg watched as she silently worked away. Her concentration seemed so complete, so intense. Like everything she did. Total commitment, no half measures.

Awg was burning to find out more about her, and tried to think of some smart way of asking. But the question that finally came blurting out was

'Isn't it working?'

Awg could have died of shame. He felt this was about the stupidest thing he could have said, like asking someone with their leg crushed under a lorry if it hurt.

The girl answered the question.

'All the functions seem to be operating but I can't get any signal. If we had another power source I could check the circuits and maybe boost the sensitivity. But there's no power in this building – everything's dead.'

She went back to work. Awg felt somehow relieved that there was nothing he could do to help. He got down from the bunk.

'Is it OK if I take another look around?' he asked.

The girl looked up.

'Yeah, that's OK. It's safe to explore the upper floors – down to the level where we came in. And you can go into the hall on the entrance level and look at the shaft where the stairs go down. Just be careful. Take a headset.'

She handed him a lightweight helmet with a lamp in front.

'But don't go down to any of the lower levels. We haven't explored all of them and there may be dangers we don't know about – perhaps even booby traps.'

The girl glanced anxiously out across the desert and then went back to working on her radio.

Awg slipped quietly from the chamber and pattered down the passage. Most of the outer rooms seemed to be lookouts like the one he'd come from. In between were larger spaces. Some had lines of dilapidated tables as if they'd been used for office workers, and one must have been a mess room for the guards. Next to it was some sort of control room with a large semicircular desk on which were rows of buttons with symbols against them.

In the centre of the desk was a black cube and Awg had the feeling it worked as a screen or display. He blew away the thick layer of dust and rubbed the surface with his sleeve. It seemed to be made of black glass and (Awg jumped when he spotted it) etched in the bottom corner was the sun symbol – the same symbol Awg had seen on the clock and on the stone at the top of Gellyn mountain. He pressed a few of the buttons near to the cube in the hope that something might light up. Nothing did. Just as the girl had told him, everything was dead.

On the next two levels were rows of very small rooms. Cells for the prisoners. They were horribly like the one he had been in at Tukzadryk.

The next floor down was the entrance level and Awg found himself at the metal door by which they had entered. They had immediately ascended a stairway to the right and, standing with the door behind him, Awg could now see an identical set of stairs going up to his left. He guessed that everything he had seen would be duplicated on that other side of the building, so that even the above-ground levels of the fort must contain dozens – no, hundreds – of rooms.

In front of him, a wide passageway led directly into the hillside. He turned on the light on his helmet and found it gave a surprisingly intense beam. He wondered how long the battery, or whatever powered it, would last.

After a short distance, Awg found himself in a large round chamber cut into the rock. In the centre, a wide shaft plunged downwards. Around its edge a spiral staircase descended into the depths. Awg went to the rail, peered over – and gasped. Level upon level upon level vanished eerily into the gloom. The shaft was so deep it was impossible to see the bottom.

Awg began to descend the stair. If he just stuck to the staircase and counted the levels as he went down, all he had to do was reverse the process and he would be back where he started. There surely couldn't be any danger on the staircase itself.

He went down five levels. On each level, passageways radiated out from the central stairway and he could see that every passage contained rows of cells. Awg shone his light down each passage in turn and tried to imagine what it would have been like when the place was heaving with prisoners. Now it was deserted. Only his own feet echoing on the stairs broke the otherwise total silence.

He went down five more levels. Level ten was different. The space around the stairway was much larger and no passages ran off from it. Instead, around the walls were what appeared to be a series of large metal cylinders, each one open at the front. Awg left the stairway and approached one of the cylinders. It looked a little less derelict than the rest. Inside was a space the size of a small room. On the wall was what Awg at first took to be a notice board. There was a vertical column of black discs and beside each one a series of hieroglyphics.

Three things then happened in very quick succession.

First, the black disc at the bottom glowed white.

Second, Awg realised what the cylinder was.

Third, there was a loud click from the left-hand side of the opening.

Awg threw himself towards the hallway as the door snapped shut and watched in horror as the lift sank rapidly downwards. He scrambled to his feet and found that his legs were shaking. He shot over to the staircase and began to run up the stairs.

He reached the sixth level. The passages ran off to the cells just as they did before.

It was the same at the fifth level. Except that there were no more stairs.

There were just no more stairs. The staircase ended. The roof above was solid rock. There were no more levels above.

Awg stared at the mass of rock in disbelief. It seemed impossible that he had miscounted. Only twenty minutes earlier he had come down ten flights of stairs and now he had re-climbed five of them. Where were the rest? His only way back to safety and the world outside had simply disappeared before his eyes.

He remembered the girl's warning. *Anything* could be waiting for him in these lower levels. Real terror seized him for the first time since he had woken in Tukzadryk.

In blind panic, Awg tore down the first of the passageways. Empty cells yawned to his left and his right. He stumbled over the door of one cell that had come off its hinges and fallen across the tunnel floor. At the end of the passage was a blank wall.

Awg ran back to the stairwell and looked wildly around. One of the tunnels seemed a little wider than the rest. He ran down it. Beyond the rows of cells, the passage bent to the left and began to slope downwards through solid rock.

Openings to caves and further passages began to appear to left and right and then the tunnel split into three. There was nothing to indicate which was the main route, so Awg carried directly on. After about half a mile the tunnel split into three again, and again he took the middle way. A hundred yards further on, the passage came to an end in an empty storeroom.

Angry at himself, Awg trudged back up the tunnel. After a long time, and certainly having walked back more than a hundred yards, Awg still hadn't reached either of the three-way junctions. Instead, he came to a place where the tunnel forked into two. Awg was absolutely sure that he'd never seen this junction before. He wondered if he was hallucinating and leant against the tunnel wall to get his breath back ...

... and fell into the hole where the third passage was.

He picked himself up and took a step forward. At once he was back at the fork. He put his hand out to touch the tunnel wall and found only empty space. The wall was a hologram.

Awg was sick with the realisation that he had been tricked. How much of what he'd been seeing had not been reality – including the disappearance of the stairs above the fifth level? He must get back there at once. But was this the first junction or the second? From the length of time he'd been walking, it must be the far one, the junction nearest to the cells. So if he walked straight back along the central tunnel, he would reach the stairwell.

But Awg never reached the stairwell, or the corridor with its rows of cells. Somewhere in his wanderings he had been diverted into a maze of passages which forked and divided and criss-crossed. At each new junction, he felt around to check what was real and what was not, but before long he realised that whichever way he chose to take, all the tunnels seemed to be going downwards. He became grimly aware that a lot of effort was being put into getting him down to the lowest level.

He gave up trying to find a way upwards and trudged on. Most of the rooms or caves he had passed had been empty but, when he had been walking for what seemed hours, he came to a room that had a table and a bunk bed in it. Awg was miserable, scared and dead tired. He'd disregarded the girl's advice about not going below the entrance level and now he was lost and probably being hunted by someone – or something. He needed a rest.

The bunk bed looked inviting. Awg was too exhausted to consider the improbability of a comfortable bed being conveniently situated right in front of him in the bottom-most level of an ancient prison that had been deserted for years.

He turned into the room.

And walked straight into the wall on which the hologram was being projected. An immensely strong, grey-skinned arm caught him as he fell and set him back on his feet.

'Do be careful now,' said a familiar voice. 'We wouldn't want yer to get 'urt, would we?'

Twenty Six

When in the eight hundredth year of the twenty-fourth Patrician dynasty it was decided to construct a new prison in the eastern desert, the imperial surveyors discovered that the deepest storage tunnels under the old fort ran out to a point less than two miles from the proposed new site. It was therefore decided to deepen and extend them to accelerate the building programme. Headings were driven out and construction was begun both above and below ground.

When Tukzadryk was completed, the upper levels of the old fort were abandoned but the links to the lower levels were maintained for strategic purposes. Several tunnels connected the two prisons. Awg's image had been picked up by an optical sensor as he entered the lift bay on floor –10 (ten floors below ground level). After that, an ancient security system had alerted the guards at Tukzadryk and shepherded him downwards and back towards his starting point. He was now in a cell on level –38 in Tukzadryk. He was not alone.

'I checked the rules on recaptured prisoners. It says they got to be interrogated.'

The zwnerba jailor felt uncomfortable. Recaptured prisoners were something out of the ordinary. Best to get on with it.

'Now them doors is pretty tough – and besides, there wasn't no damage. So either you got some gizmo what'll spring the lock or someone let you out. So just tell us what happened and everyone'll be happy. An' you better say where you got that helmet, an' all.'

He picked up his noteglass and stilograph and saw something he'd written at the top as a reminder.

'An' by the way your sentence is doubled on account of tryin' to escape. Just to let you know.'

Awg felt utterly choked off. Not only had he thrown away his freedom but he was now in possession of a dangerous secret. The guards clearly saw the cell door as the only possible escape route: somehow he'd got through it. Perhaps they were suspicious of each other. If they guessed that he had an accomplice from outside the prison – and one with a different way in – he would be betraying the girl and putting the rescue of other prisoners in jeopardy.

He tried bluffing.

'It wasn't like that. I didn't go through the door. I just felt faint and when I came round I was lying in that passage. I don't think the plasma was working properly. I think I faded.'

'Nah, nah. Come off it! You oughta know the plasma don't work like that. If the strength goes dahn for a bit then you just goes back to the receiver when it picks up again. You'd be up top of the tower, not down 'ere somewhere.'

He gave a snort.

'Course, if it goes off completely, then that's a diff'rent matter.'

'Why, what happens then?' asked Awg, hoping to find a way to wriggle out of the questioning.

'The system loses the addresses.'

'And ...?'

'Well, say you was just in the process of bein' transferred from here to another planet and the system goes down real bad. Then, all the stuff about where you come from and where you're gettin' sent gets lost. It's called "loss of coordinates". So when it powers up again all it can do is set a random destination. So you could end up anywhere – out in the void, on a hostile planet, anywhere. You'd just disappear, prob'bly for ever. People have.'

He picked up his stilograph and absent-mindedly stuck it up his nose.

'Only happens occasionally, though.'

Twenty Seven

The zwnerba stood for some minutes wondering which forms he'd have to fill in if one of his prisoners disappeared irreversibly into the plasma. Not "escaped prisoners" because they hadn't actually escaped. Not "dead" because they might be alive somewhere – at least for a while. Did the time they spent disappeared count as part of their sentence if they ever came back? There was probably a special form for it, though he'd never seen one.

Unfortunately for Awg, his jailor suddenly remembered why he'd come to the cell in the first place.

'Now, where was we? Ah yes, Stage 1. I asks you nicely to tell me what happened; then, if you won't tell me, we go on to Stage 2. For that, we got to go along to the assistance room.'

'Assistance room?'

'Yeah. If you can't recall how you escaped we got stuff there to help you remember. Now – you goin' to tell me how you got out?'

Awg decided. He wasn't going to betray the girl.

'No, I'm not,' he said. Awg had a strong feeling that this was not going to be one of his better days.

They left the cell and went up several floors in one of the cylindrical lifts. Awg was led down a maze of corridors and into a sizeable room. At one end was a comfortable-looking sofa. On a nearby table was a black cube like the one Awg had seen in the control room at the fort.

At the other end of the room was another chair – and Awg did not like the look of it at all. It reminded him of a dentist's chair in that there were various pieces of equipment mounted on stands around it. However, Awg had a shrewd idea that the various sharp instruments and electrical probes were not designed to increase the health and life expectancy of the occupant. This suspicion was further confirmed by the thick black restraining straps.

Awg was relieved to be led to the sofa. The zwnerba remained standing.

'Now,' he said, ' 'fore we starts I wants to reassure you that I've no bad feelins towards you at all. So any horrendous pain what I may inflict is purely a function of my nat'ral desire to do me duty.

'I'll explain the procedure. An' if there's any bits you're not clear on, do feel free to ask. There's three degrees of persuasion we employ – an' in order to minimise any discomfort the first step is to show you some pictures of each procedure an' its effects. We hopes o' course that havin' seen the results on the screen you'll be minded to cooperate wivout havin' to experience it all person'ly.

'Now before we begin, I 'ave to ask you to sign one o' these indemnity forms.'

He stuck a sheet in front of Awg covered in rows of hieroglyphs.

'What it says is you consents to the procedures we're offerin' an' won't hold either the Tukzadryk administration, or me personally, liable for any physical or mental injury you may suffer as a result. Purely a formality.'

'You want me to sign a form saying I agree to be tortured? That's absolutely gross! What if I refuse?'

'I dunno. I probably got to torture you till you agrees to sign it. I'll go an' check.'

He started to leave the room, then turned back.

'I tell you what. While I goes and looks this up, why don't you watch the first of the films. It'll save time.'

He reached into a drawer underneath the table and took out three black glass discs.

'See – this is the first stage. You got to watch this one first. Then, if you decides you'd like to co-operate, there's no need to be strapped in that chair and have the akshul experience.'

He bent down towards Awg, towering over him like a dockyard crane.

'That's what I'd recommend, partly o' course 'cos I'm the one who'll have to clear up all the blood an' vomit afterwards. But it's up to you. I'll put the other two films out as well, just in case.'

He was just checking the other two films over when he stopped again.

'Eh-Heh! We got a problem 'ere. On this third one it says "Contains violent and gruesome scenes. Not to be shown to under-age sentient beings." You got your adult pass-card yet?'

'N-n-n-no.'

'Thought not. Can't let you see the third one, then. We'll just go ahead wivout it, if needs be. Sorry an' all that. Gotta stick to the rules.'

Awg thought that if he was dreaming it would be a good plan to wake up quite soon.

'You mean you're allowed to do unspeakable things to me but I'm not allowed to watch a film of them being done to someone else?'

'Yeah, that's right. Mind you, now you puts it like that it does seem a bit funny. Tell you what, I'll look that up as well.'

Awg stared at his interrogator and at the nightmare chair down the end of the room. Something inside his head cracked like the shell of an egg, and all the lunacy poured out. Awg's face contorted into a hideous grin and he broke into fits of hysterical laughter.

The effect of this upon his captor was astonishing.

He fell on his knees and clasped his fingers in front of him.

'Why didn' you say? Nobody told me! O Jeblhybd! O Shrilrwst! I'll never get me Good Citizenship badge now. I'm finished.'

He took Awg's hand in a vice-like grip.

'Put in a good word for me, sir. Tell 'em I treated you proper – by the rules. Please, please!'

And he keeled over on the floor and was violently sick.

Twenty Eight

Awg gazed down upon the changing landscape. Soon, they had left Tukzadryk behind, and the dust and stones of the low hills were below them. They flew over the old fort and out across the far reaches of the eastern desert. After several hours, patches of green began to appear; at first occasionally, and then more and more frequently until they joined up into a wide expanse of rough grassland. In the distance, a dark green line drew steadily nearer, and suddenly they were flying over acres of dense jungle.

Many miles further on, the wide outline of a river wound its way beneath them, and, at one point in its path, the jungle fell back to surround a huge cleared area. Ahead lay green and brown fields of crops, whilst on the approach side was the square outline of an ancient city. Awg saw what appeared to be paved streets and stone buildings.

'That's Gexadkydubm,' said the zwnerba pilot. 'We'll be landin' in 'bout five minutes.'

He looked across at Awg.

'You should'a told him straight away. It wasn't nice for him to find out like that. Terrible shock for the poor chap. He was only doin' his job.'

From that surreal moment in the torture room, Awg had been treated like royalty and he had absolutely no idea why. He had been taken to a large and luxurious office. He had even been given proper food and drink: well, a bread-like substance and a sweet-tasting fruit drink. Then, two zwnerba guards had taken him out to a flying machine and he had left Tukzadryk behind.

The machine had a grey metal base and a transparent dome. There was a circular rotor at the top of the dome and the metal chassis had six wheels. Underneath, there also appeared to be another small rotor, set at an angle. Awg was intrigued to see whether the device would trundle along the surface, take off, or bore itself into the ground. In the event, it took off almost vertically and flew rather noisily at a height of several hundred feet.

As they drew nearer to the city, Awg's jaw dropped open as he did a double take. Below him were great pyramid temples with flights of steps sweeping right up to their tops. There were huge palaces with fantastic carvings and observatories with black stone monuments. It was just like the TV programme he'd remembered in Llangarreg when he first saw the strange triangular clock. But the buildings in that programme were in Central America, on Earth. What were they doing here – wherever "here" was?

They landed on the flat top of one of the pyramid temples. Awg got out. Two zwnerbas greeted him by bowing their heads and then escorted him down the steps and into the temple. Once inside, Awg found that the building was internally not at all like anything he had seen on TV. It was in fact more like a huge library.

'This is our Central Records Office,' said one of his guides. 'Our Director will authenticate your lineage in order to establish what honours are appropriate for you.'

Awg was taken to a room high up inside the building. Light poured in from many windows. Around the walls were hung colourful tapestries decorated with geometric patterns. They were the first things that Awg had seen since his arrival on Zero that were not purely functional.

At the single desk in the middle of the space sat a very old man. Like the girl rescuer, he could easily at first glance be taken as human. It was only when you looked again that you knew: the unusually long, narrow face; the browless eyes set just too high in the head to be believable, the ears almost level with the eyes.

As Awg entered, he rose shakily to his feet and bowed.

'Greetings, my Lord,' he said in a cracked voice. 'I hope that you will accept our humblest apologies for the unfortunate mistake which brought you to … *Tukzadryk*.'

He said the word with distaste, as if it were something he had accidentally trodden in.

'The system has never before made such an error. We will do our utmost to make amends. If you will be so gracious as to take a seat, we will begin.'

He pressed a key on a small control panel set into his desk.

'As you speak, your answers will be relayed to our researchers, who will in turn inform me of their conclusions.

'Please state your full name.'

'Allardyce Wentworth Gilhooley Bradley.'

'To which of the eleven Great Families do you claim attachment?'

'Eh? I mean 'Pardon?''

'To which of the eleven Great Families do you claim attachment?'

'I don't know. I shouldn't think I'm attached to any of them.'

The Director looked startled.

'Sector and coordinates of the planet on which you reside?'

'The Earth. I don't know the sector or coordinates.'

There followed questions about his parents, his parents' families, their dates of birth and (if applicable) death, addresses and so on. Awg could hardly answer any of it. As the questions went on, the Director appeared more and more perplexed. At the end, a screen lit up and he read the message on it.

'Well, my Lord, at least I can understand the nature of the error which led to your auto-extradition to Tukzadryk. There is no record of your name and lineage in our system. That would appear to imply one of two possibilities. Either your family is so ancient and of such nobility that it predates our records, or …'

'Or what?' asked Awg.

'I would prefer not to dwell on the alternative, for fear of causing offence to your Lordship. You must forgive the inadequacy of our record system. I shall make further enquiries. In the meantime, I shall entrust you to the hospitality of the Mayor of our city, who will look after your present needs.'

He pressed a further key on his desk console. Had Awg been able to read the screen he would have seen that it said "search for known impostors".

Twenty Nine

The Director knew very well that he had no need to make any apologies for his record system. It was in fact the largest and most comprehensive in the galaxy, containing over ten thousand billion (10^{13}) entries. So when he was unable to discover anything about Awg's ancestors, he smelt a very large rat. However, he was a cautious man who knew that no computer system is stronger than the most gullible idiot's ability to misinterpret the output. He therefore decided to buy a little time in which to make some further enquiries.

Awg was duly taken to the bijou residence in the leafy suburbs of the city reserved for visiting dignitaries and the most favoured civic guests. Exhausted by his experiences in Tukzadryk and the subsequent long journey, he fell into bed and slept soundly.

Waking early the next morning, Awg set about exploring the suite of rooms that had been placed at his disposal.

His first and most urgent need was to find the bathroom. Days of strange food eaten at irregular intervals had taken their toll of his digestive system. He did discover something but it was not what he was used to. There was no wash basin, no bath, no shower. And where was the toilet?

In the corner of the room was something which looked like a cross between a desk chair and a pressure cooker. He lifted the lid and found that it was half full of stuff like cat litter. Awg was desperate and felt he had to take a chance. He used the (with luck it's a) toilet and then shut the lid. Thankfully, he pressed the stud by the side. Nothing happened. He opened the lid again and decided that it would definitely be a good idea if he could get the thing to work. Then he found that beside the seat there was a small wheel with a handle. He wound the handle round and discovered that this pulled the lid tightly down and locked it in place. He pressed the stud again. There was a tremendous noise like a lot of marbles being shaken in a tin. When it stopped, he wound the handle back again and found that the interior was clean and dry with a new charge of cat litter.

The only water in the room was a small bottle that was clearly meant for drinking. There was also a rough cloth and a spray can. Awg squirted some of the spray on to his hand. It was cool and fresh and had a pleasant smell. The last time he had washed was in Llangarreg and he was horribly conscious of the need to see off the considerable layer of grime and sweat that had accumulated since then. There was also the residue of the stinking anti-balerid ointment. So he worked from head to foot by spraying himself a bit at a time and then drying off with the cloth. It wasn't brilliant but it was decidedly better than nothing. He was sure that anyone standing next to him would agree.

The large window in his bedroom opened on to a balcony from which there was a good view of the gardens surrounding the villa. For a moment, Awg could have imagined himself back on Earth – but only for a moment. Everything was the same and yet not the same. Plants were growing and flowering but they were not like the shapes and colours of any plants or flowers that he had ever seen before. There were very few birds and, as far as he could see, no insects. All the time he was conscious of something that should have been there and wasn't. It was only when he looked out of a side window into a small inner courtyard that he understood what it was.

In the centre of the courtyard was a tiny fountain and Awg realised that this was the first time he had seen flowing water. During his journey over the jungle, he had spotted what appeared to be a river snaking through the trees – but it had been just a curve of brown amidst the green, and since then there had been nothing, not even a sign of the smallest stream. He was beginning to appreciate what the girl at the fort had told him.

Beyond the villa gardens, Awg could see into the road outside. There were a few wheeled vehicles but most of the population seemed to get about on foot. Zwnerbas appeared to outnumber the humanoids by about ten to one. Strangely, though, it was the humanoids he noticed most because they wore coloured clothes. Awg had rather assumed that his jailer in Tukzadryk had been in uniform but it seemed that all the zwnerbas were dressed alike in similar grey tunics.

Awg wondered about his own clothes. They were not so very different from some of the things the humanoids were wearing outside, except that his were by now dirty and torn. Not exactly the smartest gear for visiting the Mayor that afternoon. However, in the room adjoining his bedroom he found that a set of new clothes had been laid out. He tried them on and found they weren't a bad fit, although he was profoundly grateful that none of his mates could see him. A sloppy green shirt and baggy pink trousers were not exactly the things he felt most comfortable in.

He went through his old pockets and tipped all the stuff out on the bed. Then he wound his clothes into a roll and tied them up with his two socks knotted together. He sat down on the bed and assessed the sum total of his possessions:

One roll of dirty clothes
One watch
One screwdriver
One stone from the top of Gellyn Mountain
One broken elastic band
One half-empty bag of peppermints

It wasn't much. He didn't know it yet, but in that small pile of belongings lay his only hope of ever getting back to Earth.

Thirty

Chief Councillor Sharibvdl had not got to be mayor of Gexadkydubm for nothing. It had cost him a lot of money.

He had started out in the time-honoured way by undercutting his shopkeeping competitors until they were forced out of business, then making a huge hike in his own prices to exploit his monopoly situation to the full. Then he had branched out into property and speculative building. He went on the prowl for easy, lucrative contracts.

Bribing the junior councillors had not proved too expensive, and as soon as they'd played ball once, it was of course in everybody's interest to do so again – and again. The one or two who had second thoughts found that interesting articles about their private lives appeared in the local news outlets.

But Councillor (elected without opposition) Sharibvdl's stroke of genius had been to plant various of his relatives in the prison administration system. If somehow a person of wealth could be tricked into breaking one of the Laws, then they would be auto-extradited into Tukzadryk or another of the larger and more remote detention centres. Then, it could be arranged that the details of their case would be lost in the system. Once they became a non-person, it was a relatively easy matter to relieve them of their identity, their property and their life, usually in approximately that order.

So when Mayor (appointed by unanimous vote) Sharibvdl was asked to play host to an unknown prince from an as-yet unidentified royal house he was more than interested. There was almost certainly money in it.

Awg was ushered into the most lavish room he had yet seen. He had rather liked the spacious office of the Director of Records, with its simple elegance and tapestried walls. It had seemed to mirror the rather austere bearing of the ancient Director himself, who had been polite and very correct, but not obsequious.

The Mayor's office also reflected the character of its odious and oily occupant. The walls were painted in garish colours with bulbous statues and hideously ornate carvings. Everything was in excess, including the waistband of the mayor himself. Awg was shown towards a pink velvet chair into which he sank like a bath, whilst the mayor bulged over him at a huge and convoluted purple desk.

'Welcome! Welcome to our humble province,' exuded the mayor. 'It is *such* an honour to receive a guest of so exalted a station in our utterly insignificant city. I understand you are from a distant planet ...

He paused, and his piggy eyes grew even rounder.

'... I expect it is a land of great wealth.'

'Not especially,' said Awg, struggling to sit up straight, 'although some people *are* very rich. The Queen's the head of our Royal Family and she owns lots of palaces and other stuff. She's loaded with money.'

This was certainly a promising start but the mayor didn't want to press the matter too much at first. It might just possibly seem greedy. Besides, he had other concerns.

'And do the people from your planet possess any unusual powers?' he went on. 'Perhaps they have special methods to protect themselves from attack – the ability to release hallucinogens from their toenails or drip plague-inducing bacteria from their earlobes?'

'Er ...well, not exactly. Some of us do judo, which can come in pretty handy.'

The mayor wasn't sure about judo but it didn't sound life threatening.

'But not telekinetic powers, for example? You can't use your mind to move objects around?'

'Er, no.'

That was a relief, then. Safe to find out a bit more.

'When are you intending to return home? Not that I'm hoping that your stay with us will be anything other then an extremely long and happy one, of course. But – when are you expected? And if you didn't turn up, would a lot of people come looking for you, possibly with weapons?'

Awg knew his parents probably wouldn't even notice he was away.

'My gran would be upset if I didn't get back,' he said.

The mayor saw his chance to return to his favourite subject.

'This GRAN – is she a relative of the QUEEN you spoke of? From whom perhaps you derive your own royal ancestry and wealth?

A bell rang, and a light sparked up on the mayor's desk. He was very annoyed at being interrupted just when the conversation was beginning to get interesting.

'Please excuse me for a moment – Council business, I'm afraid.'

He left the room and Awg sank back into his tub-like chair.

'Psstt!'

Awg looked around but could see no one.

'Psssssssssttttt! Up here. Don't trust him!'

Awg looked up.

Then he nearly died.

From high up on the wall, a spider was looking down at him.

The spider was about three feet across.

Thirty One

Awg felt suddenly unterrified. The spider was obviously not going to attack him. He also had a strange feeling that this was a young spider. Like, about his own age – in spider terms. Someone he could be friends with, like with his mates back home. But his mates back home did have fewer limbs, and only two eyes …

'OK, OK. Just get used to it! You should see what some o' the people in this galaxy looks like. I threw up when I first saw a Nerian: all them nodules an' green slime. You just gotta get used to it. An' you're in deep shit, so listen!'

Awg listened.

'The mayor – he's a crook. Why d'you think he's askin' all them questions?'

'No idea,' said Awg, 'but then I didn't know what to expect. I've not met many mayors of jungle cities in alien worlds.'

The spider clicked in exasperation.

'He's lookin' at you as a walkin' wallet. Say you mysteriously disappears on your way back to the Town House – ain't there someone somewhere who'd pay a whack o' dosh to get you back?'

'Kidnapping, you mean?'

'Yeah – that, or worse.'

Awg felt he didn't need to know about the worse.

'He wants to find out how much you're worth, whether you're dangerous or not, an' whether anyone'll be tryin' to find you.

'You shouldda told him you can burn holes in things with your eyes an' important people'll come lookin' for you with guns if you don't get back.'

'It's too late now,' said Awg. 'He can see I'm just small and ordinary.'

'Is it true you can work your face?'

'Eh?'

'Work your face – make expressions. Only the Patricians can do that. It's the way they can tell you got royal blood.'

Awg grinned, and then pulled a horrible face.

'Hey – you can! You're a star! You'll never see anyone here do stuff like that, unless you goes to the Palace.'

It was true. Now he thought about it, none of the humanoids he had seen in the city had ever smiled, or frowned, or shown anything other than a fixed facial expression. It wasn't that their faces were identical – they weren't. It was just that each one stayed the same all the time. Awg was beginning to understand what had happened with the jailor at Tukzadryk.

'So – take offence at somethin'. Do a big strop. Put on a huge scowl an' walk out. That'll scare the hell out o' him 'cos he'll think he's goin' to get it in the neck from the high-ups. The real high-ups, that is.

'An' another thing – don't eat or drink anythin' he gives you. It'll probably be drugged. That's the sort o' cheap trick he'll try. He doesn't do subtle. Not bright enough.

'Look out now, he's comin' back! If things gets rough, I'll divert him again an' give you a chance to do somethin'.'

'Again?' queried Awg.

'Yeah, it was me that rang the bell the first time. I shorted the circuit. I'm good at stuff like that. 'Bye!'

The spider shot up to the corner of the ceiling and disappeared through a large ventilator. The mayor compressed himself into his chair and wiped a bead of sweat off his forehead.

'Sorry about that. No-one waiting after all. Now, you were telling me about this GRAN person.'

Awg took a deep breath.

'Well ... yes. She's a very important person. Very GRAND. That's where the name comes from, like in Grand Duchess. She speaks to the Queen a lot. Every day, in fact. I'm the heir to her vast fortune. But the Queen has a huge army – millions and millions – and if anything ever happened to me they'd find where I was in an instant and probably launch an invasion fleet.'

Awg thought he heard a sort of choking noise from somewhere behind the ceiling. The mayor eyed him suspiciously and Awg wondered if he might perhaps have overdone things a bit.

'I think it's time for refreshment,' said the mayor. 'Shall we have some acglava juice?'

'Nothing for me, thanks,' said Awg hurriedly.

'Oh, come now – you must join me. It *might* be taken as impolite if you refuse.'

He went to a table in the corner and poured out two glasses of a yellow liquid. Awg watched him like a hawk. He saw that the drinks were taken from different vessels. One glass was placed in front of him and the mayor took the other.

Awg pretended to drink some of the juice.

At that moment there was a crash and a scream from somewhere along the corridor. The mayor put down his glass and hurried out of the room. Voices were raised and there was a scrabbling sound as the pieces of something large, fragile, and – until very recently – valuable, were swept up. When the mayor returned a few minutes later, Awg was sipping appreciatively at his drink. The mayor noted that he had drunk over half of it. He picked up his own glass and emptied it at one gulp.

'This is rather good,' said Awg. 'I'm very glad I tried it. Where does the juice come from?'

'We make it from the fruit of the acglava cactus. It grows at the edge of the desert but we also cultivate it in the city gardens.

'The fruit is crushed in special presses and the juice is collected. We make it from the fruit of the acglava cactus. It grows at the edge of the desert but we also cultivate it in the city gardens.'

Awg sat up sharply. The mayor was looking decidedly odd. He was sitting completely still and his eyes were glazed.

'Where does the juice come from?' asked Awg again.

'We make it from the fruit of the acglava cactus. It grows at the edge of the desert but we also cultivate it in the city gardens.'

The mayor gazed fixedly at nothing in particular.

Got you, thought Awg. Truth drug. He had switched the glasses while the mayor was out of the room. If the mayor was going to try cheesy tricks, Awg was up for it too. And he was going to twist the knife a bit.

'Just exactly how did you get to be mayor?' asked Awg.

'It took a long time, but I discovered some simple rules,' said the mayor in a flat voice. 'The first is, walk over anyone who is no use to you. On the other hand, cultivate those who can advance your career: find out what they most desire – money, sex, or whatever – and give it to them; then extract the maximum possible payment in return. It's best to get some sort of intimidating hold over them, so if you want to ditch them they can't get back at you.'

His hand, resting on the desk, shook slightly.

'Another good rule is always to do the absolute minimum in your day-to-day work. You can usually find some other sucker to do it, or at least to shift the blame on to if it goes pear shaped. It's all about power, really. Now I've got to the top, I do exactly as I like. I even set my own salary – suitably enormous, of course. But it's peanuts to what I get by fixing contracts and siphoning off the money into my own companies. No one can touch me because they know I'll get them drawn into prison. That's especially satisfying because then I can rob them as well.'

He stopped as suddenly as if he had been switched off. Awg decided to have one more push.

'But what about the higher authorities? Don't you think they'll rumble you sooner or later?'

The mayor sniggered.

'What higher authorities? The Patricians? That's a laugh. The old families're finished. Washed up. They'd better look out. Soon it'll be New-Patrician Sharibvdl and his family who call all the shots. Yes. Yes, Oh yes, yes ...'

The mayor slid from the chair into an untidy heap on the floor.

'Good thinking, man! You did well! That's nailed him.'

Awg looked up at the spider. He was getting used to it.

'Yes, but it's only us that heard it all. I wish I'd had a tape recorder.'

'Wossat?'

'A machine that writes sounds on to a magnetic tape so that you can play them back to someone else.'

'No sweat. I done that.'

'What! You recorded all that stuff – all he said?'

'Yep, every word. It'll keep a while. I knows what to do with it. Trust me. Now you better leg it back to the Town House.'

'What about the mayor?'

'Don't worry. When he wakes up he won't remember nothin'. 'Fore you goes, swap the glasses back – jus' in case anyone checks up.'

'Who are you?'

'Jus' a technician. A trainee-technician to be exact. The Director sent me to keep an eye on you.'

'The Director?'

'O' the Records Office. He suspected you was a phoney from the start. He's a smart guy.'

The huge spider sidled further down the wall until it was just a few feet away. It quivered slightly and the hairs on its ebony-black, jointed legs glistened.

Awg swallowed uneasily. He still hadn't got completely used to it.

'You're from Earth, ain't you?' said the spider, very quietly.

Awg was absolutely gobsmacked.

Earth. Someone had actually heard of it. Earth. Just to hear the name again. Earth. His mates at home. His gran, Llangarreg. He found his eyes filling with tears.

'Yes, YES! I'm a person from Earth. How did you know?'

'I seen one before,' whispered the spider.

Thirty Two

Awg spent a restless night. He couldn't get the spider's words out of his head. It had seen someone else from Earth. So had the spider been to Earth – or had the person been here on Zero? Both seemed equally unlikely. Awg also wondered how much of his dealings with the mayor had been reported back to the Director of the Records Office.

And what about these Patricians? The girl at the old fort hadn't mentioned anything about *them*. From what she'd said, the government system was run by a sprawling network of zwnerba administrators. Now it seemed there was a family of Royals as well.

He got up as soon as it was light. A supply of food and water was always left for him, so he dressed, had a quick breakfast and went out. He wanted to explore. The zwnerba on night duty looked up from his desk but said nothing: there was no instruction that the boy should not come and go as he pleased.

Awg walked through the gardens surrounding the Town House and out to the road. In one direction he knew that it led back to the old city, so he set off in the other. There were very few people about and, apart from the occasional stare, no-one paid any attention to him. He felt a complete pillock in his green shirt and baggy pink trousers but at least they made him look enough like the other humanoids that he didn't stand out. He just hoped that no one would study him too closely.

The road began to climb and Awg found himself ascending a small hill. On the top was one of the stone observatory towers he had seen from the flying machine. There were no signs which might be saying *keep off*, so Awg tramped up the spiral ramp to the top, where there was a flat platform with a stone plinth at its centre. From here, Awg could get a panoramic view of his surroundings.

The city of Gexadkydubm was divided into the old and the new by the sweep of the river. The old city itself with its labyrinth of narrow streets and box-like flat-roofed houses fitted snugly on the inside of a great bend, whilst stretching out along the banks up and down stream (but on the same side) were the oldest suburbs. Across the river, a large and unsightly urban sprawl had, in more recent times, given the old city a new and ugly twin.

Below and away to his right lay the green and brown fields of crops he had seen from the air. Awg knew that these had been straight ahead as they had flown in, so he could use them to get some idea where he was. His flight from Tukzadryk had been more or less on a single bearing all the way, and they had passed directly over the old fort. From what the girl had told him, he knew that meant they had been flying due west.

It was early morning and the sun (just one) was to his left. So if he assumed that, as on Earth, the sun rose in the East, that would tie in with the fields of crops being over to the west and on his right. It made sense. Pheeew!

But there was definitely something funny about those green and brown fields. Awg wished he had some binoculars. He strained his eyes to make out the detail and eventually realised that the squares weren't fields of soil. The crops appeared to be growing in huge rectangular tanks. And the sun wasn't the same as the earth's sun. It was much bigger and much redder.

Around the hill, a park-like suburb spread southwards to the boundary of the old city. Awg could easily pick out the Town House and he could see that there were other rather grand houses dotted here and there. The ground was mostly covered with a thick-leaved, greenish grass and there appeared to be two different types of trees. The smaller, pyramidal ones seemed to have hardly any leaves but were covered in clusters of coloured spheres. Whether these were fruits in different stages of ripening, or something else entirely, it was impossible to tell. From a distance, they looked absurdly like decorated Christmas trees. Towering over these were trees resembling desert palms, their tall, thin trunks ending like feather dusters in a plume of blue foliage.

A road led out of the old city across a three-arched stone bridge, the broad central span traversing the whole river. At each end of the bridge were gatehouses with towers. Awg had seen this river from the air, as it snaked its way through the jungle towards Gexadkydubm. What had been hidden from his aerial view, but was now all too plain to see, was that he was looking at a ghost, a great waterway of the past. The bed of the river was completely dry and its banks were rock and dust. On its far side, where the withered jungle had shrunk back from the dead river, lay the new city of Gexadkydubm. Acres of rectangular buildings were laid out on a grid pattern. There were no trees.

Beyond the square outline of the old city, hemmed in by the tightening curve of the dry river, was another area of green. This was much smaller than the expansive northern suburb and at its centre was a single building. Awg looked at its elegant courtyards and spacious gardens and wondered if this might be where the Ruler of the City lived. In this he was correct: it was indeed the centuries-old palace of the Patricians of Gexadkydubm. What Awg did not guess was that in a few hours from now he himself would be inside it.

Awg felt it was probably time for him to make his way back to the Town House. The streets were beginning to fill with people and there was always the chance that he might be singled out. You didn't have to look so very closely to see that he was different from the humanoids. On Zero, *he* was an alien.

Almost at once, his fears were realised. A group of young humanoids saw him come down the ramp from the observatory. Perhaps people weren't supposed to go up there, after all. Perhaps it had some religious significance and he had committed an act of disrespect, like not removing your shoes in a mosque. He could see the group huddled together, talking and gesticulating. Suddenly, they turned and came for him.

Awg fled down the path and along the road. He was a good runner but his pursuers were gaining on him, bearing down in a cloud of street dust. Awg dodged down an alleyway and hid amongst a stack of tall grey containers. He thought he was safe but one of the gang spotted his shoe sticking out. They kicked at the pile of containers which toppled over, spilling their contents of muck and garbage into the alley. Awg bolted out from the stinking mess and ran into a yard between the houses backing onto the alley. A zwnerba came out to see what all the noise was about. Awg sprinted across the yard and into the alleyway on the opposite side.

Surrounded only by walls and houses, Awg lost his sense of direction and blundered out of the alley into a larger, and unfamiliar, road. However, the land to his right seemed very flat so he guessed that the observatory hill was somewhere behind him. He had just turned to look when the gang appeared round the corner. They whooped in triumph at finding their prey again and came racing towards him. He hammered down the road. Awg was getting tired now and two or three of the gang were catching up fast. When they were only ten yards away, the leader slipped his hand inside his shirt and brought out something metallic that glinted in the sunlight. Awg didn't wait to see what sort of weapon it was. He was running alongside a head-high wall: he jumped for his life, got his fingers well over the top and swung himself up. He straddled the wall and dropped down the other side. He found himself in a small courtyard. In the centre was a tiny fountain: he was in the garden of the Town House.

Awg dived inside and collapsed on his bed. It was the same everywhere. Look a bit different and you're in for trouble. The faces of the gang might have lacked human expression but the eyes had said it all. Awg had seen the hate and it had scared him. Perhaps some things – like the basic pack instinct of animals – were universal. But he was glad he'd gone out. At least he knew a bit more about Gexadkydubm. And he knew that Gexadkydubm was on Zero.

But where was Zero?

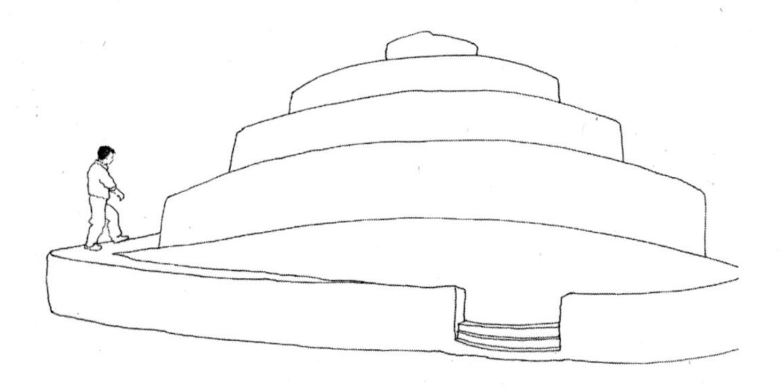

Thirty Three

The Director of the Central Records Office waited until Awg had returned to the Town House. Thanks to the mutronic tag sealed into the lining of Awg's pink trousers, he knew exactly at what time Awg came back and precisely where he had been. Since the previous day, he had been busy on Awg's case. He understood very well that Awg was not a young lord from a nearby planet – his investigations had ruled that out conclusively. The boy was also clearly not an impostor, in the sense of a criminal adventurer looking to con them out of money or property. He seemed honest and genuine and had asked for nothing.

That left only one possibility. After all these years, it had happened again. The Director inscribed a message to the Patrician and sent it to the Palace by special courier.

Meanwhile, back at the Town House Awg had made an interesting discovery. In an alcove between two of the rooms in his suite was something which looked suspiciously like a kind of communication system. On the top was one of the black cube screens he had seen before, and below this was a small platform on which were traced the outlines of fingers. At one side was a switch which could be pointed towards three sets of symbols. The first looked like a house, the second a group of many houses, and the third a scroll with hieroglyphic writing on it.

Awg guessed (correctly, as it turned out) that the first position communicated to rooms within the Town House itself, the second with other locations in the city and that the scroll represented a directory. Awg set the pointer to the information position and placed his hands on the platform.

The cube began to glow and a line of hieroglyphic symbols appeared on its surface. Awg groaned in frustration as the thought *What the hell is that supposed to mean?* went through his mind. Immediately, the display changed. It now said

ASK YOUR QUESTION

Awg was so startled that he looked round to see if anyone else had come into the room. He was then horrified to discover that he could still see the words in front of his eyes, apparently imprinted upon the air – even though he was no longer looking at the screen. He snatched his hands away from the machine and the writing disappeared.

So it was like the module things in his ears. Somehow, the machine translated the meaning of whatever language was on the screen – presumably Zeroian – into symbols he could understand. But the scary part was that the translated symbols weren't actually on the screen – they were in his head.

Awg was torn between his curiosity to use the machine and the fear that it might do something bad to him, like burn up his brain. It wasn't built for humans and you never know what might happen. After a few moments he decided that he hadn't suffered any harm the first time and decided to give it another go. He placed his hands back on the platform.

ASK YOUR QUESTION

The words re-appeared.

This device was obviously rather more than a telephone directory, so Awg decided to ask it stuff he really wanted to know.

'Where is planet Zero?' He spoke the words out loud.

PLANET ZERO IS [00,00,00,00]

'Yes, I know. But that's not what I meant. I meant *where actually is it?*'

PLANET ZERO IS [00,00,00,00]

Awg decided to try something else. Also, he didn't say the words this time. He just thought them.

'What is a Patrician?'

It worked just the same.

THE PATRICIAN IS THE HEAD OF THE RULING FAMILY OF THE PLANET ZERO. ALTHOUGH THERE ARE MANY THOUSANDS OF INHABITED PLANETS IN THE GALAXY, ZERO HAS THE OLDEST CIVILISATION AND IS GENERALLY TAKEN TO BE THE CENTRE OF ITS ORGANISATION AND GOVERNMENT.

IN FORMER TIMES, THE GALAXY WAS RULED BY VARIOUS MEMBERS OF ELEVEN WARLIKE FAMILIES WHO GREW TO CONTROL FIRST THEIR OWN PLANETS AND THEN THOSE NEARBY. EVENTUALLY THE PLANET MYRFIGIXIUS CAME TO DOMINATE ALL THE OTHERS. MYRFIGIXIUS WAS RENAMED ZERO AND BECAME THE MILITARY AND ADMINISTRATIVE CAPITAL OF THE GALAXY.

THE PATRICIANS OF ZERO PROVED TO BE WISE AND FAIR RULERS WHO ENCOURAGED PEACEFUL TRADE AND THE PURSUIT OF LEARNING. UNDER THEIR GUIDANCE, THERE WAS A BLOSSOMING OF SCIENTIFIC AND CULTURAL LIFE.

EVENTUALLY, A GREAT ALLIANCE WAS FORMED BETWEEN THE NATIVE ZEROIANS, THE ZWNERBAS OF SALHINOR AND THE SPYRIDI OF OSPIROS. THIS AFFILIATION ENDURES TO THIS DAY. THE SUCCESS

OF THE PARTNERSHIP IS FOUNDED ON AN EXTENSIVE GOVERNMENT ADMINISTRATION RUN BY THE DILIGENT AND BUREAUCRATIC ZWNERBAS, BACKED UP WITH SOPHISTICATED TECHNOLOGY PROVIDED BY THE SCIENTIFICALLY GIFTED SPYRIDI.

THE PATRICIAN OF ZERO CONTINUES TO FULFIL THE ROLE OF HEAD OF STATE AND, WITH A RULING COUNCIL, IS RESPONSIBLE FOR OVERALL GALACTIC POLICY.

*

At around mid-day, Awg was very surprised to receive a visit from the Director himself. What he had to say surprised him even more. Awg learned that the Patrician of Gexadkydubm wished to see him.

'I have to tell you that this is very unusual,' continued the Director. 'Few people are invited for an audience these days.'

Awg felt seriously uneasy.

'I haven't any gift or message for him, and I've only got my old clothes and the ones which the people here gave me. And it's all a mistake. I'm not a prince or anything, and I never said I was. I'm just a completely ordinary boy. I can't be of the slightest interest to him.'

'On the contrary,' said the Director. 'You are of the greatest interest to him. And the more you say, the more I believe that everything you have told us is true. Zert certainly thought so. He liked you.'

'Would Zert be a sp... I mean, your technical assistant?'

'Yes, that's right. He told me the mayor dozed off in the middle of your conversation with him. I'm so sorry. His civic duties must have exhausted him.'

The Director ushered Awg outside where one of the six-wheeled heli-vehicles was waiting. This time it didn't rise into the air but trundled off down the road. Awg couldn't help wondering why a civilisation which had apparently mastered the transport of matter through space still used such a utilitarian method of getting about. It was like as if someone owned a Ferrari but rode about on a pushbike. But as he asked himself the question he also began to guess the answer – although he did not yet understand how very strange part of that answer would turn out to be.

The curious vehicle rattled through the crowded, narrow streets of the old city, clattering over potholes and lurching around the sharp corners. The only open spaces were those around the pyramid temples. Awg recognised one of them as the Records Office and wondered what the others were used for, or if they were used at all. The ordinary houses seemed to be of two types, one much smaller and squarer than the other. Awg eventually realised that the taller and more angular buildings were where the zwnerbas lived. Humanoids needed rather less space and could use lower doorways.

'Why do you think the Patrician wants to see me?' asked Awg.

The Director thought for a moment. 'You represent something new, something different. The galaxy has enjoyed peace and prosperity for a very long time and the Patrician is constantly on watch for anything that might threaten its stability. He fiercely resists any suggestion of change. Even to raise the possibility is seen as an act of treachery. So it is partly curiosity and partly caution. You should remember this and be careful in what you say.'

The helicar swerved violently to avoid an elderly and very bent-over zwnerba who emerged from an alleyway pushing a cart loaded with purple fruit. Eventually, they stopped at the gates of the palace gardens which Awg had seen from his hill a few hours earlier. Apparently the vehicle was not allowed beyond the entrance, so Awg and the Director got out and began to walk up the avenue to the palace itself.

Awg started to get nervous. Surely he was not seen as some sort of threat? The Director's comments had not exactly been reassuring. What did the Patrician really want? What was he going to ask? Awg began to dream up answers to possible questions, like "What do you think of our world?" or "Describe three things that have happened to you." For some completely mad reason, he began to think of it all in another way, like what he would say if he wrote a postcard home to his mother:

Dear Mum

Sorry I've not written before but I left a bit unexpectedly. When I woke up, I found I was in prison. Luckily I escaped and didn't get frizzled by the death ray but then I nearly got devoured by flesh-eating rats. A girl helped me but thought my leg was too hairy. Then it all went wrong and I got captured again. I was just going to be tortured to death by an eight-foot alien when I pulled a face and he threw up. Then they thought I was a prince and flew me over the jungle to a city with Mayan temples. I nearly got drugged by a crooked mayor but this time I was saved by a giant spider. Sorry I've got to go now because the King wants to see me. The weather has been very nice which is good because I haven't got an anorak.

Love
Allardyce

Thirty Four

Awg walked with the Director through the gardens and into the palace. The Director progressed slowly and creakily and Awg had plenty of time to take the measure of his surroundings. Everything was very fine, in a gloomy sort of way. There was none of the showy gaudiness of the Mayor's residence. The colours of the stonework were sombre, the statues and carvings grim and austere. Where the walls had tapestries, their colours and patterns were subdued. And there was something else. There was hardly anyone about.

A few zwnerbas were tending the gardens but overall there was an air of neglect. The outer walls of the palace were pitted and flaking, and weeds grew through cracks in the stone paving of the avenues. Inside, as Awg was led from empty hall to empty hall, it seemed as if the building belonged so firmly to the past that it was discomforted by the tread of any intruders from the present day.

In one of the rooms through which they passed was a glass case surrounded by a rail. Awg stopped to look at the object on display. It consisted of three bronze-coloured metallic spheres joined together by a silver rod. The central sphere was much larger than the outer ones and was about the size of a cricket ball.

'What's that?' said Awg.

'That's a piece of history,' said the Director. 'Take a good look – you'll never see another like it.'

He joined Awg at the rail.

'In the early days of plasma transport, there were many accidents. The apparatus was new and very complicated. People were killed, or vanished without trace.'

'Was it because of "loss of coordinates"?' asked Awg, remembering what the Tukzadryk jailor had told him.

'Yes – that, and also the physical danger. Sometimes the time and space mapping was inadequate, or the details became corrupted in the extraordinary complexities of those first machines. On other occasions, the intensity of the plasma field itself proved fatal.

'A way was found to minimise the risk. They developed a resonator which amplified and concentrated the effect of the plasma field. Those who carried the token you see there were virtually certain to reach their destination safely: the probability was said to be ninety-nine point nine percent. And because most of the energy passed through the resonator, the stresses on the voyagers' bodies were also much reduced.

'But there was a problem. The resonator required an extremely rare metal – iridonium – for its core. Not only that, the metal had to be arranged in very thin layers – many thousands of them. The device took them over three years to construct and in the end only two were ever made. One was sent on a research mission and was lost. That is the other. It is priceless.'

'Why is it here?' asked Awg. 'Shouldn't it be in a museum or something?'

'The iridonium resonator is kept here because the Patrician wishes it. It is an heirloom of his House. I suspect also that it gives him a feeling of security. Should some disaster overtake the planet, he knows that there is a certain escape route for him or his successors.'

At last they came to a small complex of rooms in the east wing which seemed to be more in use. Awg began to feel increasingly jittery. He was wondering more and more about the Patrician's motives for inviting him into his domain. What if the palace had dungeons, or stuff like that?

A single zwnerba appeared and spoke quietly to the Director before going on in front of them. The Director in turn halted briefly and whispered to Awg.

'When he greets you, bow your head slightly – and do not sit down unless he asks you.'

They entered a spacious, octagonal chamber. The Patrician was seated in a single, high-backed chair of carved black wood. He was tall and gaunt, and wore a flowing, dark red robe. On the floor was a carpet of the deepest crimson into which were woven beautiful and intricate patterns in fine, white thread. Otherwise, the room was bare of all furnishing and decoration, save for a pattern of hieroglyphs inscribed, high up, around the white stone walls.

The Patrician raised his hand in greeting. Awg bowed.

'Please walk,' ordered the Patrician, indicating the space in front of him with a sweep of his arm.

Puzzled, but wanting to do as he was asked, Awg trotted around in a wide circle and then did the same in the opposite direction, coming to a stop in front of the Patrician again.

'I wished to see the young person from planet Earth. We shall talk. You may sit.'

The zwnerba brought a small chair and placed it in front of the Patrician. Both he and the Director then left the room.

Awg sat down. The Patrician bent forward towards him, so that they were only a few feet apart. He spoke in a whisper, his pale face cratered and wrinkled as if carved from driftwood.

'Why have you come?'

Awg was stunned. Of all the questions he had thought he might be asked, this one had never entered his head. Answering it was going to be awkward. Especially the bit about the prison ...

'There was no particular reason – it was ... an accident.'

'An accident? I wonder.'

The Patrician was silent for a while, then leaned closer still.

'Who has sent you? If you are a messenger, then what is your message and from whom do you bear it?'

Awg felt guilty and uncomfortable, as if he were in the room under false pretences. Something was expected of him that he didn't understand and couldn't deliver. But he knew that he had nothing to say except the bare truth.

'I'm afraid I don't have any message. I got here by accident and no one sent me.'

The Patrician's eyes searched Awg's face. 'Time will tell,' he said. After a long pause, he added 'Do you love your planet?'

The question again took Awg by surprise. It wasn't something he'd thought about very much. Now, sundered by a seemingly unbridgeable distance, he pictured his favourite places, especially Llangarreg – and knew the answer at once.

'It's my home, and I do love it – very much.'

'Yes, it is a beautiful place. Your sun is yet young. There are still rivers, seas – you are indeed fortunate.'

The Patrician appeared lost in thought. Awg wondered how he knew these things.

At length, the old man roused himself once more.

'Do you know what is written there?' he said, gesturing upwards to the stone inscription.

'No,' said Awg. 'I can't understand the symbols.'

'It is the Oath of Office of the Patricians of Zero, set into the fabric of this room as a daily reminder to each one of us. I swore

To dedicate my life to the service of Zero and its Galaxy
to strive for truth and fairness in all my actions
to uphold the Rule of Law without fear or favour
and to seek no personal reward.

'I swore this, as did my father, and my father's father, and so back to the ancient days. It is our great tradition.'

Awg was beginning to get over his nervousness and to feel an increasing curiosity. It was not every day you met someone who ruled a whole galaxy, and Awg thought he would like to know more about how it was done.

'Is it permitted for me to ask a question?' he enquired, hoping that this was the right thing to say. It was obvious you couldn't come straight out with something like "What do you do all day?" although this was actually what he wanted to find out.

'It is permitted.'

So far so good.

'It must be very difficult to rule a whole galaxy,' Awg continued. 'How do you keep in touch with such a huge number of people?'

The Patrician settled back in his chair and appeared to unwind a little. Awg also relaxed. Only slightly, but it was still too much.

'My rule is achieved through the Galactic Council. There are representatives from each of the major planets. Our principle task is to decide Galactic policy on vital matters such as the provision of energy and the sharing of natural resources.'

'And matters of Law?' queried Awg, thinking of the inscription and of his own experiences in Tukzadryk.

An alarm bell should have rung in Awg's head. He was now treading on dangerous ground.

'As the affairs of the Galaxy have become ever more complex, in one aspect the life of a Patrician today is easier than that of his distant ancestors,' continued the old man. 'For generations now, Patricians have no longer had to burden their minds with the administration of justice. Once laws are established, our scientists have given us the means to uphold them with complete impartiality. The system is swift and needs no input from living beings. It is therefore infallible.'

'But machines can make mistakes too,' blurted out Awg. 'No one can build a machine that never makes a mistake. Where I come from computers are always doing stupid things.'

The next moment, Awg remembered the Director's warning – but it was too late. The transformation in the Patrician's manner was immediate and terrifying.

'You betray your ignorance!' he raged. 'You do not know for how long this system has been tested. In hundreds of years it has never failed. It is *treason* to suggest that the faith of our illustrious ancestors was misplaced – that they were mistaken.

Do you think for one moment that *you* are wiser than they? It is as well you are my guest!'

And then it was over. The Patrician sank back, his hand trembling.

'I apologise for my anger. You cannot be expected to understand.

'Look around you at this great building. It is old and strong. Our system of government is like that. It has served us well for centuries – and will do so for centuries to come!'

Awg cast his eyes around the room. He thought it would be unwise to point out that there were cracks in the walls. Although shaken by the Patrician's outburst, he was beginning to feel sorry for this lonely man in his crumbling palace. And so he was quite unprepared for what happened next.

The Patrician stood up and clapped his hands. The zwnerba returned to the room, spoke briefly with the Patrician and disappeared down a long corridor.

'There is someone I wish you to meet,' said the Patrician. 'I have no sons. But I am fortunate in having a daughter who knows her duty to me and will not question our traditions nor disobey the rules for preserving them.'

Awg heard voices in the distance. He was not looking forward to meeting the Patrician's daughter, particularly if she was as prickly and aloof as her father.

As the sounds came nearer, Awg could hear a voice that was as intense as the Patrician's was weary, as fervent as his was cold. A voice that sparkled with energy and interest. A voice that he could not believe he recognised. And his mind flashed back to the morning in the old fort when the girl joked about the fur on his body and pulled down the leg of his jeans with a wicked smile on her face. The words went round and round in his head. *A wicked smile on her face.* At the time, Awg hadn't seen anything unusual in a smile. But now he did.

Thirty Five

Awg foresaw what was about to happen and psyched himself up for it. The girl came into the room. No longer kitted out in her grey desert tunic, she was dressed in a red robe like her father. She greeted him, turned, and saw Awg.

Her blanched face contorted with terror. The scream that was on her lips was already ringing in Awg's head. The Patrician would start forward in shock; the girl would spin round to face him; she would betray herself.

But the scream never became a reality. With a huge effort of will, the girl atomised it into a million silent fragments that danced around the room as harmlessly as specks of dust in a projector beam. Awg remained impassive, and slowly the girl realised that he wasn't going to say anything, do anything – that he was in control, and that her terrible secret was safe.

The Patrician was unaware of the drama being played out only a few feet away. By the time the girl turned to face him again, she had regained her composure. Awg gazed at her with what he hoped would seem innocent interest.

'This is my daughter Asa,' said the Patrician. Awg rose from his chair and bowed.

'She will accompany you to Auyvhasdh. There you will learn about your journey to this planet and its importance to us.' His hand moved in a gentle arc: a courteous but unmistakable gesture of dismissal.

'I bid you farewell,' he said. Their audience was at an end.

Asa bowed to her father and slowly withdrew. Awg nodded

his head respectfully and followed. At the door, he paused for a moment and looked back. The Patrician sat alone in the near-empty room, remote and motionless in his tall, black chair. He seemed to have withdrawn from the world around him just as completely as he had withdrawn from their meeting.

Awg followed the Patrician's daughter through a succession of corridors and empty halls. He hurried forward to catch up with her.

'Why didn't you ...?'

Awg's question was cut short by an icy glare from Asa.

Almost at once they emerged into a large courtyard at the back of the building. At its centre was a white-painted landing pad on which one of the helicars was waiting. It was smarter and in a better state of repair than the others Awg had seen, and sported a broad red stripe around the grey metal base and across the transparent dome.

As soon as they appeared, the zwnerba pilot started the engine. Without a word, they climbed inside and were soon airborne. They flew westwards over the tankfields of crops. Looking back, Awg could see the old city with its narrow streets and pyramid temples, and he could just make out the observatory hill where he had climbed early that same morning. It seemed an age ago.

Suddenly, Awg realised that he was still wearing the new clothes that he had been given. His old ones – together with his few possessions – were back at the Town House! It was obviously too late to return for them now. Compared to being gnawed to the bone by desert rats or tortured to death it seemed a small loss, but he felt saddened that yet more of the things that connected him with home had been stripped away.

Awg had expected their flight to be a long one and was surprised when after only a few minutes they began to descend again. They landed at a small airfield where about a dozen of the heli-vehicles were drawn up in rows. There was a small conical control tower, an open hangar and what seemed to be facilities for re-fuelling.

As they left the plane, Asa spoke in a low voice to the zwnerba pilot and Awg was astonished to see that they then embraced warmly. As he himself went forward to get out, the zwnerba extended the fingers of a silver-grey arm towards him. With some misgivings, he held out his hand, whereupon the zwnerba touched it lightly, at the same time nodding vigorously and adding, 'I am a friend. I have done some work for you. Good luck.' The zwnerba handed him a large brown box. Awg tucked it under his arm and jumped down.

Asa led the way to one of the parked helicars. This one was as grimy and battered as most of the others he had seen and was clearly not any sort of official vehicle. Awg waited for a pilot to appear but it was Asa herself who fastened the cabin door and took the controls. Only when they were again airborne did she speak to him for the first time.

'That was Berjga. She's completely loyal to me. I've known her for many years.'

'She?'

'Yes. Female zwnerbas look to us very like the males, although they're usually not quite so tall.'

Asa increased the speed of the engine, locked the vehicle on a north-easterly course, and darted a fierce glance across to Awg.

'Now – we've got to talk! I want to know what happened at the fort. You were stupid and disobeyed my instructions. And how did you get to Gexadkydubm? And I want to know who you've been talking to and what you've said about me.'

Her tone was unfriendly and aggressive, and Awg was hurt.

'OK,' he said indignantly. 'How much did I blab to your father?'

She bit her lip. 'No,' she said. 'That was impressive.'

'And I haven't said a single word about you to anyone else, either! You were brave. You rescued me. And I'm *not* stupid!'

As they flew on, Awg told her all that had happened since they had got separated at the fort – about being recaptured, the assistance room, the journey across the jungle, the meeting with the mayor.

'So even when you thought you were going to be tortured, you didn't give me away?'

'*No*. But if he'd really got me in that chair I might have. That's what scared me most. I might've said *anything* once those sharp things and the electric shocks got going. It was horrible.'

Asa was silent for a long time. Finally she said, 'I'm sorry. Not many people could have done what you did.' She leant over and punched his side. 'But I still say you were an idiot to go down into the lower levels at the fort when I warned you not to!' The tension was broken.

'You know my name now. What's yours?' asked Asa.

'I don't like my real name. My friends call me Awg.'

'Then you shall be Awg to me.'

'Thanks. Do I have to call you "Your Highness" or anything?'

'Only if you want a broken arm.'

Awg laughed. 'You told me that Berjga was loyal to you,' he said. 'But I thought the whole point about the zwnerbas was that they lived entirely by the rules – and you certainly don't!'

'Berjga is unusual, but she has good reason to be,' replied Asa. 'Her son was tricked into breaking one of the Laws and got sucked into prison. We don't know where he is, or even if he's still alive. We're doing all we can. So Berjga can see that the rules aren't working fairly any more, and she understands that some of us are trying to do something about it.'

'So there are zwnerbas stuck in prison as well as ...'

Awg was about to say "as well as humanoids".

'... as well as people like us?'

'Yes, of course. The same Laws apply to everyone. And as the zwnerbas greatly outnumber the other two peoples, it follows that there will also be more of them in prison.'

'Surely your father must know all this?' said Awg, puzzled. 'How can he possibly ignore it if he truly believes in justice?'

'He ignores it because it is *convenient* for him to ignore it. To acknowledge the failures would mean facing up to too many hard truths. It's more comfortable to maintain the illusion that the time-honoured system is perfect. Even if a part of him suspects the truth – that everything has changed – he can't bring himself to admit it.'

'And I suppose that suits some people very well – the ones that are creaming off a fortune at the moment and don't want anything to upset their scams and deceits.'

'Exactly! Most of his advisors are as corrupt as mayor Sharibvdl and tell him only what he wants to hear. They do all they can to reinforce his belief that everything is right and as it always was.'

'But – you're his daughter. And he's obviously proud of you. Can't *you* get him to see reason?' Awg asked his question cautiously, but Asa's despairing response still startled him.

'Do you think I haven't tried?' she said, angrily. 'Time and again I've started to discuss a problem and he's cut me off. He won't listen to the argument and refuses to look at the evidence. He's certainly proud of me – as a trophy to show off! He has such a fixed idea of what I should be that he is blind to what I am.'

'Then what about the other Patricians – this long line of rulers that people talk about. Can't all the rest of his great family do something?'

'You don't understand. There *is* no great family any more. He's the last of the line. *He's the only one left.*'

Thirty Six

'The only one left?' said Awg in amazement.

'Yes. It is hard – for everyone. There are so many expectations. Is it possible to be both faithful to the past and committed to the future? And all the time knowing that if I fail, then our House will truly be at an end.'

She glanced across to Awg. For a moment, despair again showed itself on her face. Then she tossed her head with the flick of defiance that Awg remembered from their time in the desert, and her eyes regained their fire.

'But at Auyvhasdh I can be myself,' she said. 'We'll be there soon.'

After taking off from the small airbase, they had flown at first over more of the strange, square tankfields that Awg had seen on the western outskirts of Gexadkydubm. Having left these behind, they were passing once more above a wilderness of rough grassland.

Awg watched Asa as she deftly operated the controls of the helicar. 'When did you learn to fly?' he asked, wondering secretly if there was anything that Asa *couldn't* do.

'I learn everything I can. When you live as I do, you never know what ability or skill you're going to need next – and your life may depend on it. Besides, these old transporters are very primitive – it's not hard to operate them.'

She showed him the basic controls: rotor pitch and angle, engine speed and thrust, autopilot. At first it seemed very complicated, but as they flew onward he gradually saw how it worked and which lever controlled what.

They began to cross increasingly large areas of barren scrub until the treeless plain beneath them had degenerated into semi-desert. Awg could see high ground in the distance. One hill had a very flat top with some sort of spike in the middle.

'That's where we're going,' said Asa.

'Auyvhasdh. Is it a town?' asked Awg.

'It's a city; a very special community. It's where our scientists and philosophers live and work. The name means "haven of learning".'

'I can't see any streets or buildings,' said Awg.

'No, you won't. There's nothing there.'

'I thought you said it was a city.'

'It is – but it's not visible.'

'So it's underground, you mean?'

'No. Strictly speaking, it's not on this planet at all. It's located inside a large volume of interstellar space that's been condensed down and contained. The whole thing's connected to Zero by hyperspace links. One way to reach the city is the one we're about to take, but there are others. It's a way of protecting our most vital technology in the event of disaster. If Zero were devastated by asteroid impact, Auyvhasdh would relocate itself somewhere else.'

By this time they had reached the top of the flat hill. Awg took one look. He closed his eyes and clutched at his seat. He must be dreaming. Awg looked again.

The top of the hill had been quarried away to leave a completely flat space. The surface of the ground was covered with something that looked like bright silver tarmac. Around the extreme edge, a white metal rail ran in a circle, passing at regular intervals through small silver domes. But it was none of these things that had shaken him rigid.

In the dead centre of the space was the spike that they had seen from a distance – now revealed as a huge, shining, ebony-black pyramid: a reminder on a vast scale of the clock at Llangarreg. And on each of its sides was the sun-like symbol that Awg had first seen on the clock's face.

'The central point's the antenna,' said Asa. 'The resonance ring around the edge defines the extent of the plasma field.' She landed the helicar in the open space and taxied over until they were only a few yards from the base of the pyramid.

'Now we wait. They're expecting us, so it won't be long. By the way, some people find this experience alarming.'

At first, nothing appeared to be happening, but then Awg became aware of a slight vibration throughout the aircraft. At the same time, the light began to fade and the outlines of objects outside seemed to be getting indistinct. As it grew darker, the wall of the pyramid became translucent and began to expand outwards, then dissolved completely like mist clearing from a mirror. Their vehicle was being absorbed into its depths. Awg became aware of an abyss opening beneath them. He braced himself. Surely they must fall? But there was no sense of movement. The blackness closed in above and around them. There was total darkness and total silence.

The space around them became brighter, and for a while Awg could see thousands of images of their vehicle receding into the distance in all directions. And brighter still, until the light was blinding, and there seemed to be out-of-focus spherical shapes all around them. Gradually, the glare faded, and the shapes resolved themselves into a geometric pattern. They were again on a flat surface, in the centre of a circular space, and all around them were low, domed buildings connected by tubular walkways.

By the side of their vehicle was a metal post carrying a transparent globe from which an intense blue light was shining. Awg sensed it was some sort of warning. Asa followed his stare and nodded.

'Plasma indicator. Residual field's still high at the moment.'

She pointed across at the pattern of spherical buildings, which Awg could now see stretched away far into the distance. 'This is the city of the Spyridi. They created all this, and much more besides.'

'The Spyridi?' queried Awg.

'The third of the three peoples of the Great Alliance. They are the foremost scientists of the galaxy: the greatest inventors, the greatest innovators. Surely you saw their symbol on the sides of the antenna when we arrived at the mountain? They put it on everything they make. It's the signature of their technology – their trademark, if you like. It represents their people and their culture.'

The colour of the light in the globe changed from iridescent blue to a soft yellow.

'Safe to go outside now,' said Asa.

As they climbed out, a three foot high spider came across to greet them.

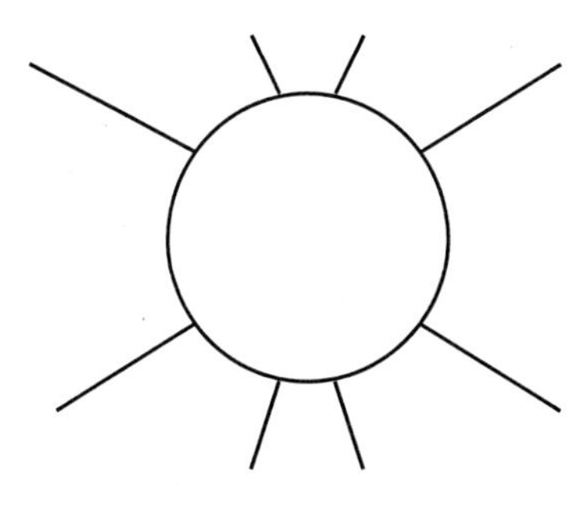

Thirty Seven

'Hallo Zert,' said Asa. 'Does Xurog know I'm here?'

'Nope. Not yet, anyhow. I coded your transfer *orange-3-1* so you're in the log as "staff relocation – miscellaneous". He'll prob'ly find out, though. He always does.'

'Can you look after Awg and show him round?' continued Asa. 'He needs to meet Xurog and Garik but that can wait until we've found him somewhere to live.'

Asa disappeared inside one of the spherical buildings. Zert started off along a surfaced pathway and beckoned Awg to follow.

'Gettin' used to it yet?' said Zert. 'The Commander knows we met before. She's good, ain't she? Very focused. Her guys'd do anythin' for her. Think o' the pressure she's under. You wouldn' wanna be her. No way. Notice she didn' say, "This is Zert. He might look a bit weird to you but he's OK." She's grown up with it an' you just gotta get the same way.'

'Where I come from,' said Awg, 'there's only one sort of people. Well, there's loads of different shapes and sizes and colours but they're all basically the same.'

'Yeah. So there's no competition for jobs. You got so used to thinkin' you're the only smart creatures. Now, say you're not feelin' too good an' you goes to the doctor. But when you gets there, the doc turns out to be some sort o' supersize frog. What woulddya think?'

'It'd be seriously weird – but I suppose I'd listen to what it had to say.'

'You *bet* you would. An' if you lived in a place where all the best medics was ultrafrogs, then you'd just accept it. You'd get used to it.

' 'Course, sometimes there's problems. That's why sentient beings that're on the squidgy side tend to stay put on their home planets. Last year, a load o' Huvians come here for a conference. There shouldda been publicity so everyone knew. Now, Huvians is *mighty* squishy, an' a bit on the small side. Well – a group of 'em had oozed along to a corner. They'd got a bit lost an' stopped to look at a virtual street map. Then – whaddya know – some zwnerba street cleaners come along, mistook 'em for a chemical spillage, an' flushed 'em away down a drain.'

They had arrived at a square which appeared to mark the boundary of the sphere-and-tube structures. Across the other side was a park-like area which, apart from the peculiarity of the plants, could almost have been taken for a scene on Earth. In the distance were several groups of large buildings.

'This is the college,' said Zert. 'You'll feel at home round here. They made it like the planet used to look 'fore it started dryin' out.'

'I saw the same sort of trees in Gexadkydubm,' said Awg.

'Yep – but they only keeps it like that by havin' pipes an' stuff under the ground everywhere. They gets water every way they can, mostly from what's left deep under the jungle an' from the salt pools where the lakes used to be. They even makes some by burnin' hydrogen from the gas under the desert.'

The college buildings seemed to be constructed in a bewilderingly varied mixture of styles and were of widely differing sizes. Awg presumed this was a reflection of the need to accommodate a similarly varied selection of students. Just how did you manage a population of people with such a range of heights, forms and number of limbs?

'I gotta go back in a bit an' finish typin' my project,' said Zert. 'I gotta report on the work I done in the Records Office.'

'You type – actually type – on a keyboard?' asked Awg.

'Sure – why not?'

'It's crazy. You're a people that can transport matter through space and yet you have noisy old crates like those helicars – and now you say you use keyboards. Can't you just stare at something and the information gets stored?'

'Nah, nah, nah. You ha'n't thought about it. You gotta choose the technology that's most suitable for the use.'

'You mean, "Horses for courses?"'

'Wossa horse?'

Awg explained.

'Yeah – that's neat, then. 'Xactly!'

'I sort of guessed that all the stuff like the helicars was zwnerba technology and the more way-out bits like matter transfer came from somewhere else,' said Awg. 'Now I know where.'

'Yep. Them helicars is real ol' bangers, but they work an' they're reliable – so why use somethin' more complicated? Besides, there's other things you gotta think about. Matter transfer's dangerous an' don't always turn out how you want.'

'So is the typing thing the same?' said Awg. 'Used for practical reasons?'

'Yes an' no. It's a bit of a special case. Years ago, they started with buttons an' keypads an' that sort o' thing. Then they went over to voice activation. That was a mistake. Imagine a room full o' students all tryin' to write up their notes. Terrible. So then they converted to direct thought activation – but that was worse. The machine registers 'xactly what you're thinkin'. Just imagine. A guy is writin' about how to solve some equation an' suddenly a very fit female walks past – or the other way 'round. What comes out o' the machine ain't all mathematics an' is mighty embarrassin'. So they went back to keyboards. Mind you, it's got advantages for some people.'

'How d'you mean?'

'Have you *any* idea just how fast I can type with eight arms?'

They reached the end of the college buildings and sat down on some steps.

'This is where I live while I'm at school,' said Zert, nodding towards a group of dome-and-tube buildings behind them. 'My room's in there. Wouldn't be very comf'table for you, though. I'll getcha a room in the Zeroians' bit. You can live there an' get to know some o' the others. You'll soon settle in.'

Awg sat up in alarm.

'How do you mean "settle in"? It's only until I can get back home.'

'Home?' said Zert. 'D'you mean home to Earth?'

'Yes, of course.'

Zert shuffled about uncomfortably.

'Sorry,' he said. 'I thought you'dda found out by now. Your auto-transfer can't be reversed. This is your home now. You gotta live here on Zero with us. There's no way you can go back.'

Thirty Eight

Gexadkydubm, at night: the outskirts of the city. Four young Zeroian humanoids cautiously make their way towards a grey stone building at the corner of a quiet street. They are dressed in grey combat gear but are unarmed. Within a few hours, two of them will be dead.

The building itself displayed no features of interest. It was small and square with a flat roof, and the weathered stonework suggested that it had been there for a long time. The single metal door carried a green notice stating *Government Property – No Entry*. However, the simple lock made it obvious that there was nothing of value inside – and this was, quite literally, true.

The blockhouse still fulfilled its original function – but times had changed. Inside, the structure had been fortified with an inner core of reinforced pacstone. The door was lined with micronian plate and was now protected by electronic locks and a sophisticated alarm system. Otherwise, the small inner room was completely empty. Except for the manhole cover in the floor.

On reaching the building, K1 and K2 pulled off their backpacks whilst K3 and K4 took up strategic positions at opposite ends of the street.

In the control room deep inside the distant city of Auyvhasdh, the commander waited for news. She was more than usually anxious: two of the members of K-cell were close friends.

'K-unit at target. All clear. Standing by.'

K1 glanced around so that Asa could see for herself through the camera in his headset. She replied immediately.

'K1 registered. Go.'

K1 took four squares of a plastic material from his pack and fixed one to the centre of each of the outer walls. K2 locked on using the master-computer in his own pack. The thousands of sensors in the four plastic arrays allowed him to construct a complete three-dimensional map of the building. K2 located the alarm system, analysed the signal it was sending back to its base and blocked it. He then transmitted an identical and permanent 'all clear' signal in its place. A further scan of the blockhouse located the electronic locks and released them.

K1 and K3 now changed places, K3 joining the others at the building and K1 melting into the shadows opposite.

K3 inspected the lock on the outer door. Taking a set of micro-tools from the pocket of her tunic, she opened it in seconds and without the slightest damage. The outward appearance of the structure was now just as it had been before they started work.

K4 left his post at the end of the street and joined the others inside the blockhouse. From his remote vantage point K1 signalled to base: 'Building disarmed. All clear. Request permission to enter.'

Asa checked that the communication channels were all open and secure.

'K1 confirmed. Go.'

Asa fixed her eyes on the black screencube. Through K1's headset camera she watched the three others enter the building. The door closed. All she could see now was the empty street. This was the worst sort of mission. Friends risking their lives to check out a suspicion. A hunch. An idea that might at last provide some solid evidence. But at what cost?

Inside the building, K2 detached a small module from his control unit and set it in the corner of the room. This would maintain the false 'all clear" signal for the duration of their investigation.

It took two of them to pull up the manhole cover. A cold draught blew up the shaft and into their faces. Steel rungs descended into the darkness.

Their descent seemed interminable. Their arms and legs ached. At some points, rungs were broken or missing and K2 called up to warn the others following behind. Eventually, echoing up the narrow shaft, they at last detected the sound of what they had come to find. Below them, their lamps shone down on to a ribbon of running water.

Constructed when the great river began to fail, the aqueduct tapped springs deep beneath the withering jungle. As the drought intensified, the centuries-old watercourse became the principal supply for the Old City. Now grown larger and with a sprawling industrial suburb, Gexadkydubm was desperately short of water. And there were those who were making a killing by providing an illicit supply.

At first, Asa had tried legitimate means to find out what was going on. Official figures appeared to show that there was no loss from the main aqueduct. But the estimated quantities of water on the black market were so great that no other source seemed possible. An undercover investigation had to be carried out.

The main pumping and distribution station in central Gexadkydubm was too heavily guarded. However, between the centre of the city and the source of the supply the ancient builders had provided many access shafts. Most of these had since been sealed; but a few, heavily fortified and alarmed, had been retained for essential maintenance. These provided a possible way in.

From the bottom of the shaft, the three members of K-cell made their way downstream. The most likely place for any illegal access to the water would be between their entry point and the city centre.

The watercourse was in most places an open channel cut through solid rock with a narrow path at its side. However, where the ground was porous or the roof unstable there were piped or tunnelled sections. Here, the access path was forced to take a separate course and the passage of the water was hidden from view.

K2 now put on a special headset and began to use a hand-held scanner. Working on beams of different wavelengths, it measured the cross section of the channel and the average velocity of the water at the same point. From this, he got a reading of the total flow.

K4 was logging their progress. So far, they had covered half the distance between their access point and the city end of the aqueduct. They had passed two short piped sections and a longer tunnelled section. K2 had found no significant variation in the amount of water being delivered. They were now in the passage running alongside the longest tunnel on the aqueduct.

When they emerged on to the following open section, the nature of the rock had changed. The previous reddish-brown colour had become a dark green-black and it was much harder to judge the flow of water by eye.

K2 was immediately suspicious. Any discrepancy here would easily go unnoticed. He walked down the path and checked the flow at three different points. The three readings agreed with each other almost exactly but were only around seventy percent of the values he had measured previously. Somewhere in the tunnel, a third of the water was being lost. Somewhere in the tunnel.

They had been prepared for this. K3 and K4 put on miniature sub-aqua sets. There was air for eight minutes, which was judged to be enough to get through the longest tunnel on the watercourse. And this was the longest tunnel.

It was decided that K3 and K4 should go in from the downstream side and enter the tunnel against the current. If they were to swim with the flow, they might be carried past their objective without noticing anything unusual.

Although the current was not swift, they found their upstream progress much harder then they had expected. By the time they had reached the half-way point, they had used up five minutes worth of their air. So when they found a huge break in the wall of the tunnel, they were more than glad to escape into it.

They surfaced in a large open chamber. The beams from their headsets swept around the space. To their right, a wide ledge rose above the water level. Hauling themselves out, they sat with their legs over the edge. They were surprised to see bubbles breaking the surface of the water. But perhaps it wasn't too unusual: if the bottom of the pool was muddy, maybe a few bubbles of methane might be expected. But this was more than a few bubbles ...

K4 reported on their progress. Since going underground, they had been out of direct touch with base. K4 had to use a sub-terra link to K1, who could then relay coded messages back to Asa.

K3 took an instrument from her tunic and did a check on the atmosphere: no nerve gas or other toxic agents. Gratefully, they took off their BA sets and breathed in large lungfuls of the cold air. But it wasn't air.

K4 stood up and began to look around the chamber. Almost at once, he began to feel dizzy, and within a few seconds he collapsed. Alarmed, K3 moved to help him. She never even got to her feet.

Thirty Nine

K2 listened to the reports from the others, relieved that his friends were safe. And the team had successfully located the point of the water escape!

He waited for the message that they were on their way out. When it didn't come he tried to contact them.

Nothing.

He tried again, more urgently.

Nothing.

Except his own fear and panic.

But then his training kicked in. By the time he had reported back to K1, he was icy calm.

But underneath his cool ran a terrifying certainty that his team mates were dead. And that whatever had killed them now lay in wait for him.

K2 put on his own breathing set. He walked quickly upstream on the by-pass path and dived in at the mouth of the tunnel. The current carried him down towards the opening that he now knew to be there. He swam through, and surfaced in the deadly chamber. With his air supply still in place, he crawled over to where K3 and K4 were slumped on the ground. A quick check showed that they were beyond all help. Sick to the pit of his stomach, he took K3's monitor.

Check-1 for toxic agents: negative.

Check-2 for oxygen level, the test she had failed to carry out: zero. The chamber was filled with an inert gas, probably nitrogen. Perfectly harmless as long as there was also sufficient oxygen present. Stiflingly deadly if there was not.

He had been hoping against hope that his gut feeling was wrong – that, after all, his friends were unharmed. Perhaps the communication modules had got smashed or waterlogged. Perhaps K3 and K4 were stranded somewhere, but alive. Now that he knew the truth, hatred boiled up inside him. Hatred against those who had set out to steal the city's lifeblood and had set such a deadly trap for their pursuers. He wanted to crush them, destroy them, blow them into a million fragments and spit their smoking ashes far into space. He knew what resources Asa could command and he knew that it could be done.

But he also knew that this was not the way. To strike blindly against an almost unknown foe would serve only to make their own side more vulnerable. Theirs had to be a waiting game: a probing of secrets, the slow but inexorable assembly of evidence. Then, and only then, could they undermine their enemy's house of deceit and bring it crashing down.

Yet, before setting out down the tunnel, he had, through K1, asked Asa for something.

Clearance for Direct Action.

Very rarely requested and almost never granted.

But, on this occasion, clearance had been given.

By swimming in with the current, K2 had saved himself three minutes worth of air. He now had six minutes to decide the fate of his comrades' remains and get out himself.

He spent two minutes exploring the chamber and recording visual images. The water cascaded into a central cistern from which it was clearly being pumped up to the surface. Three large-bore pipes disappeared through holes in the rocky roof of the cavern. The whole installation had been there for some time, perhaps ten years or more. It was certainly not new.

If he left the bodies where they were, or cast them out into the main stream, sooner or later they would be found and identified and the team's mission discovered. The lives of others would be at risk and Asa herself in even greater danger.

He would have to adopt a course that would cover their tracks as completely as possible. This was his own speciality.

Spyridi technology gave him the means. He could already see the possibilities in his plan of sabotage. And he had four minutes in which to carry it out.

First, he sprayed the pipe assembly with a can of ultra-corrosive paint. This was a combination of acids and peroxides which would eat through any normal metal of construction. But it would look as if the pipes had just rotted away with age.

Then he fired several capsules of gel up into the exit point of the pipes. These burst on impact, covering the roof at its weakest point with a culture of some very unusual bacteria. Multiplying in cracks and fissures, they would expand into clumps of iron-hard nodules which would split the rock into fragments. In a few hours, it should bring the whole roof down, burying everything – whilst appearing to be a natural cave-in. With luck, the damage might prove impossible to clear.

K2 now had less than a minute left on his breathing supply. He plunged into the pool and struck out into the main stream. The effort cost him a lot of air. A sudden fall in pressure told him that the cylinder was almost exhausted. To conserve oxygen, he kept all movement to a minimum and let himself be carried along with the current.

Emerging at last into the open channel, he struggled to the side of the watercourse. Wedged securely against the rock, he tore his mask off and gasped for breath. It was several minutes before he could haul himself out. His first task was to contact K1.

Shortly afterwards, Asa received the message that K1 and K2 were away from the target and heading back to their lay-up point. She was white and shaken. Success of a sort – but two more deaths. And one of them K3.

K3. Brave, clever Jarça.

A warning note sounded on her console.

A breach of the secure network has been detected. The integrity of recent transmissions cannot be verified.

Asa winced. This was the last thing she needed. And it was not the first time that this had happened. Her system was supposed to carry the highest level of security and reliability. Her own life, as well as the lives of others, depended on that. She *had* to be able to rely on it. What was going on?

Almost simultaneously, a message came in on one of the back-up channels.

Security alert. Chykideyh data relay station. Unauthorised personnel detected in J-compound. Investigation underway. Await further reports.

Forty

Back in the virtual city of Auyvhasdh, Awg was sitting in his new quarters, his head in his hands.

He knew that in many ways he'd been lucky. Very lucky.

He was alive.

He'd got friends. They'd got him a brilliant room.

But nothing eased the pain he felt from Zert's words. *This is your home now. You gotta live here on Zero with us. There's no way you can go back.*

His unexpected journey from Llangarreg to Zero had been on a one-way ticket.

Awg got up and went over to the window. It spanned almost the whole length of the wall and looked out across what seemed to be playing fields. He was on the top floor of the humanoid students' block. That was to say the native Zeroian students' block – as opposed to zwnerbian Zeroians and spyridian Zeroians. And of course the native Zeroians were originally Myrfigixians when the planet had its old name. Things tended to get a bit tricky in the name department.

Zeroians. Myrfigixians. Zwnerbas. Spyridi. The astonishing nature of his new situation began to lift Awg's spirits.

He started to wonder what a game of five-a-side football would be like with mixed teams of Zeroians, zwnerbas and spyridi. With all those arms the spyridi should be in goal, that was for sure. Actually, they'd be great as forwards as well. You'd never get the ball off them.

There was a knock on the door.

It was Zert.

'You left this in the transporter,' he said, handing Awg a brown box. 'An' you gotta go an' see Xurog this afternoon. He's the boss o' the whole works. He's scary.'

'Are *you* scared of him?' asked Awg in surprise.

'Put it this way: it gives me a headache just tryin' to *think* about some o' the stuff he's done. He invented the beacons. That's how we knows things about your planet – and about loads o' others as well, as a matter o' fact. He discovered the proximity principle.'

Zert saw the look on Awg's face.

'I'm gonna have to explain, ain't I?'

Awg nodded.

'Imagine you're a rock. Or some other big solid object. Not livin', like a tree, and it don't work with liquids, so you can't be a lake or anythin'.'

'OK, I'm a rock.'

'So – whaddya do all day?'

'I sit there like a rock.'

'Don't anything happen to you?'

'No, I'm a rock.'

'Wrong. You gets warm in the sun. You gets wet in the rain. You sees daylight an' darkness. Maybe some bug crawls across you. Your surface does some chemical thing with the oxygen in the air. That's what Xurog realised – that you gotta time axis an' you're a sort o' mirror to what's 'round you. You're diff'rent from one moment to the next. Ever so slightly, but different.'

'So what?'

'So what if a way could be found to capture your 'xperience an' beam it through space. What wouldya have then?'

'A sort of sensor, I s'pose. Like the thing that detects heat in a fire alarm.'

''Xactly! You'd have a beacon. An' Xurog *did* find a way to do all them things. We got thousands o' beacons, bringin' us information from all over – even from your planet! When we're lucky – an' after stacks o' computin' – we can get to build up a picture, like a photograph. But it's like a photo with a very long 'xposure, so there's no detail o' movement or anythin' like that. Just a sorta average. But you'd be amazed at what we *can* see. It's awesome. I'll show you some time.'

He got up.

'S'long for now. See you 'safternoon.'

Awg sat down on his bed and opened the box. Inside were his Llangarreg clothes and a small fabric bag. His jeans, tee shirt and hoodie had not only been cleaned but the holes and the rips had been carefully mended as well. He tore off the green shirt and pink trousers. Standing there with his own gear on again, he suddenly felt different – and a whole lot better. He loosened the neck of the bag and shook its contents out on the bed. All his possessions were there: the screwdriver, his watch, everything – even the peppermints. Stuff from Earth. He felt he could face anything now, even Xurog.

*

Awg had expected to be shown back to the huge complex of domes and tubes near the arrival station, but instead he was led across to the centre of the college complex. There he was taken down into the depths of a building and into a room like nothing he had ever experienced before – if indeed it was a room at all. Perhaps the concept had little meaning in a city which was itself a compressed bubble of outer space. The enclosure was spherical and its walls were transparent. All around them was the night sky, dazzlingly bright with stars. In the centre of the room was a control console, and at the console was Xurog.

Awg had to a large extent got used to Zert. Looking at, walking with, talking to – and joking with – a creature resembling a spider as big as a table was not an everyday experience for most boys from Strenton. For someone with less courage and determination than Awg, it might have been rather off-putting. Especially the glistening hairs on the multiply-articulated legs, and the unusually large head with its single and compound eyes. But Awg had got used to it. However, meeting Zert had not prepared him for the full reality of Xurog.

Xurog was more than twice the size of Zert. He was as black as ebony and his eyes were red. He towered above Awg, who stood in front of him, transfixed.

'You have been brought here for a reason,' said Xurog. 'You will not be harmed. We wish to explain to you where you are. Only then will you appreciate why you cannot return to your own planet.'

'Please,' said Awg, in desperation – he couldn't wait for any explanation – 'Is there no way I can get back to Earth?'

Xurog dimmed the lights until the room was illuminated solely by the enveloping sky.

'Look out upon our Universe!' he exclaimed. 'Sun succeeding sun, galaxy upon galaxy, star after star.

'Where do you think your sun and your Earth are in that infinite sea of matter?'

Awg gazed wildly around.

'I … I don't know,' answered Awg, in a small voice.

'They are nowhere.'

'Do you mean they've been destroyed?' cried Awg, fear and panic welling up inside him.

'No,' replied Xurog in a voice of ice. 'They were never there.'

Forty One

Xurog saw the horror which had overwhelmed Awg's face.

'Do not be afraid,' he said. 'In a little while, you will understand. You look out upon our Universe in wonder. Would you be surprised if I told you that I also look in wonder – *at yourself* ? You are amazing to me. We owe a huge debt to you and your kind.'

Awg sat cross-legged on the floor and listened. He took some deep breaths and forced himself to concentrate.

'Long ago,' continued Xurog, 'many of the beings in our galaxy developed sufficient technology to become aware of one another. They looked beyond their own worlds and discovered that other life forms existed on the planets around them – and even on more distant planets around neighbouring stars. In due course, spacecraft travelled from one planet to another.

'What happened next is a lengthy and complex story but I expect that you can guess some of it. As the different peoples met, good and bad things happened. On the positive side, people became less inward looking and enjoyed the new opportunities in culture and outlook which they found. Scientists discovered new fields of research. But, of course, there were also fears and rivalries, deceptions, struggles for territory and resources.'

'And wars?' asked Awg.

'Yes, even wars, I'm afraid,' said Xurog.

'However, in the end a disaster loomed which threatened to overwhelm them all and forced them to their senses. Our nearest suns are old stars, far older than your own, and gradually all their dependent planets began to change – to change and to die. The surface temperatures rose and daylight levels fell. Crops failed and the smaller planets like Zero began to lose their atmosphere, and especially their water.

'At first, the various peoples struggled with the problem on their own, but it soon became clear that they would have to cooperate to survive. Every planet was using up its energy resources far too fast and the resulting pollution made things even worse.

'The Zeroians were the most skilful politicians and strategists, although they were hopeless at most everyday matters. So they formed an alliance with the zwnerbas, who were methodical and had the best practical skills, and ourselves, the spyridi, who had the most advanced technology. This Great Alliance has worked because it is of mutual benefit and no party has sought to dominate the others. The Zeroians have been allowed to preside overall because they rule justly and they are not corrupted by power – or, at least, the House of Patricians was not.

'The great work with which the spyridi were charged was the mastery of energy resources. There is abundant energy in the universe from countless stars – and what better than the vacuum of space through which to transmit it? The challenge was how to capture the energy and relay it to the places where it was needed. It was a daunting task but at length, after much effort, we succeeded.

'Now, you know that matter and energy are equivalent?'

'Yes, Einstein's equation, $e = mc^2$,' answered Awg, pleased to find something he knew about. 'The mass can be small, but the multiplier, *c*, the speed of light, is so huge that the amount of *e* that comes out is enormous. And it's *c squared*, so the energy is even enormouser – I mean, more enormous.'

'Yes. Good. So, matter is really a highly condensed form of energy. And as we had solved the problem of harnessing and transporting vast quantities of energy, we quickly realised that the same methods could be applied to the transmission of matter – and plasma transport was born.

'Our initial attempts were very clumsy and led to many failures and – I regret to say – tragic accidents. Some people were killed by the stresses on their bodies and others were lost into the void when the transfers went wrong. The machines were huge and difficult to control. But, eventually, we improved the procedure until it became more reliable and could be used in special cases for transportation across large distances of space. But it was still dangerous and cumbersome, and clearly far from ideal.

'And then, something completely unexpected happened, which totally revolutionised the entire technology and laid the foundation for the efficient and comparatively safe procedure we routinely use today.'

'So what did you discover – a new form of energy, or something like that?' asked Awg.

'No, it was something far more astounding. We discovered another Universe!'

Forty Two

'This is what happened,' said Xurog.

'A new and even larger plasma transport machine had been built. The amount of power required was so formidable that even our own scientists had doubts about controlling it. The building the equipment occupied would have taken you an hour to walk from one end to the other.

'We were about to transfer a team of people and their equipment from this planet to another. The personnel were prepared and the plasma generators run up to their full power. Then, the beam was energised and the transfer took place. Everything seemed to have gone to plan – but when the plasma chamber was opened, it was not empty. Our people and their equipment had indeed gone – but in their place was a strange creature, an alien from another world!

'What did it look like?' asked Awg. 'Where had it come from?'

'It was very strange,' said Xurog. 'We were afraid of it at first. But then we learnt to communicate with it, and discovered that not only did it possess intelligence but it displayed great wisdom and a depth of learning. It became one of our most valued advisors and was even invited to join the Patrician's Council. We named it Garik.

'And as to where it had come from, that took us a very long time to determine, a very long time indeed. But it led to perhaps the most important discovery we have ever made, the discovery of the Dark World.'

Awg wasn't sure whether or not to ask about this. It sounded seriously spooky.

'This solved two problems for us,' continued Xurog. 'The first was a purely scientific one: we had lost some of the Universe! It is possible to work out from gravity measurements just how much matter there should be. When we did this, we could identify where most of it was, but a small amount – just five percent – was missing. Our calculations were very accurate, so we were sure that it was not an error. We called the missing mass "Dark Matter", and we had no idea where or what it was.

'From what the creature was able to tell us, it became clear that the planet from which it came was not in the known Universe. We eventually realised that the missing five percent of mass was due to a second Universe, interwoven with our own but invisible to us: the Dark Universe. Eventually we worked out how this could be. Have you heard of something called a neutrino?'

'It's an atomic particle, isn't it?' said Awg, dubiously.

'Yes. It has no mass, no charge and half a spin – so it's rather hard to imagine! Well, it turns out that our neutrino is slightly different from the one in the Dark Universe. Only very slightly, but that tiny difference is responsible for the separation of the two worlds. They exist independently and neither can observe the other. Yet here was a creature from the Dark World! We had accidentally opened a channel of communication.

'This led to a development of great practical importance. The existence of the Dark Universe enabled us to solve the last remaining problem with our energy and matter transfer system. You will remember that by this time we had a working process, but it was inefficient and clumsy. The reason for this is rather complicated to explain – there is a technical difficulty connected with the phase of the coordinates. However, we realised that if we used the Dark Universe as temporary storage space, the problem disappeared.

'So now what we do is to transmit matter and energy in small bundles from the source into the Dark Universe, and then out again to its destination. If we use these two steps, the phase problem vanishes: the whole system and the equipment necessary can be reduced to a fraction of their former size. It was the most important single advance we have ever made. That was nearly a thousand of your Earth years ago, now.'

'And what happened to the creature?' asked Awg.

'I think you should see it,' said Xurog.

'Its bones, you mean?' said Awg, with a shudder. Then he thought of the Nerians and wondered if it had any.

'No, the creature itself. It is still alive. Come with me.'

He led the way out of the room. As they passed along the corridor, Awg was so intrigued at the thought of seeing a thousand year old alien that he forgot to be afraid of the forbidding bulk of the great spider-like creature clicking along at his side. He was indeed getting used to it.

At the entrance to the building, Zert was waiting. Xurog spoke to him in a low voice and then turned to Awg.

'Farewell for the present,' he said. 'I promise that things will very soon become clearer to you.'

Once they were safely out of earshot, Zert turned excitedly to Awg.

'How d'you get on? Ain't he awesome? Did he explain how he solved the time-transfer matrix? It needed a whole new branch o' maths to do it!'

'We went through a lot of stuff,' said Awg. 'I think he tried hard to make it simple for me and I understood most of it. But I still don't know why I can't go back to Earth.'

'Trust him,' said Zert. 'He believes if people knows the reasons for stuff they don't get so uptight 'bout it. So it can be a bit slow. But you'll see!

'I'm to take you to Garik. Asa was s'posed to come but she's bin called away. Security problem at Chykideyh.'

'Where's that?' asked Awg. 'Is it in a different part of the city?'

'Nope. It's 'bout three hours flight away. Chykideyh's our main receiver station. Sort o' information highway where signals from beacons an' special transmitters gets picked up. There's all sorts o' strategic stuff. Valuable information. Looks like someone's broke into the high-security compound that's got all the aerial arrays. Never happened before, so Asa's gone to suss things out. She looked real worried when I saw her at the transporter terminal.'

They crossed an inner courtyard to where a small building stood on its own, surrounded by a well-kept garden. The house had a pitched roof and slit-like windows, and was quite unlike any other building that Awg had seen for a long time. They went inside. The only items of furniture were a narrow bed, a table and a chair. The creature was seated at the table, reading a book. It looked up as they entered.

'Hello,' it said.

'Oh … ' said Awg.

He tottered over to the bed and sank down, his legs shaking. '… Hello Benedict.'

Forty Three

'I had a feeling we would meet again,' said Benedict.

Awg looked up apologetically, hardly able to believe his eyes.

'Sorry,' he said. 'I was expecting to see some sort of wrinkly splodge.'

'No,' said Benedict. 'I am a human from Earth, just like you.'

'Are you really a thousand years old?' asked Awg.

'Who can tell? Certainly, I first arrived here nearly a thousand years ago, in Zero's reckoning, and I have seen many generations of Patricians come and go. But how old am I on Earth? I was born in 1361 and first met you in ... which century was it?'

"The twentieth,' said Awg.

'Yes, that's right – the twentieth. Towards the end of it, I think. The trouble is, I missed out a lot of the years in between.'

Benedict sighed. 'It's all rather complicated, I'm afraid.' he said. 'For instance, what year is it on Earth now? If Xurog is right, the question has no meaning. Each of the worlds exists in its own time and the two are not connected.'

Awg wished Zert had stayed around to help with the explaining: somehow he had a knack of making difficult things seem easier to understand.

The monk smiled at Awg's puzzled expression.

'Are you feeling better now?' he asked.

'Yes, much,' replied Awg. 'Seeing you was such a shock. I thought I was the only one here.'

'And I believed the clock had been destroyed in the fire. You really should not have tinkered with it, you know. Nobody realised that the automatic imprisonment process would work outside the galaxy. It's certainly not meant to.'

'Asa was sure I'd come from a local planet when she found me in Tukzadryk,' said Awg. 'And she didn't mention anything about you.'

'My own arrival was so long ago now. No one imagined such a journey could be made again.'

'But how *did* you get here?' asked Awg, in bewilderment.

'I came on a star.'

'Seriously?'

'Perhaps I should say 'with a star'. I was on Gellyn mountain. We sometimes kept vigil up there. On this particular night there was a wonderful display of shooting stars. Suddenly, I heard a screeching sound from the sky and a bush near me exploded into flames. I was terrified and ran away. But later, as it got light, curiosity overcame me and I went back.

'Most of the bush had burned away and there were just a few of the larger branches left, blackened and still smouldering. Underneath, I saw a black stone. I tried to pick it up but it was still very hot and burned my hand. I managed to roll it into a small hollow where water had collected, and so cooled it. Then I gathered it up. It was very heavy. I was still holding it when the whole world around me became transparent. For a moment I could see through rocks and trees as if they were made of glass. The next thing I remember was waking up here.'

'Did you think you'd been dragged down into Hell?' asked Awg, fascinated.

'Yes, that is *exactly* what I did believe at first. Surrounded by astonishing sights and terrifying beings, how was I to think otherwise? I had led a cloistered monastic life. We had no technology more complex than the water wheel or the making of clay tiles.

'The people here – or "creatures" as I thought of them for a long time – were very interested in me. My appearance eventually enabled them to make a big discovery, as Xurog will have told you. So they treated me well and gradually I learned to trust them. You know what they call me here? Garik. That's because when I first came to my senses I kept saying "Llangarreg, Llangarreg ..." and they thought it was my name.'

'They spent a lot of time analysing the meteorite – for that is what it was – which I was still clutching when they found me. They discovered it had an unusual layered structure and contained a very rare metal.'

'Was it ... um... iridonium?'

'Yes – that was it. How did you know that?'

'I saw the resonator thing in the Patrician's palace.'

'So that is where it went! I often wondered. It was the meteorite that gave them the idea. But they also discovered something else – they found my meteorite had a memory!'

'How can a stone remember things?' asked Awg.

'In the same way that a patch of mud retains your footprint. The iridonium layers concentrate the plasma field. That's why I'd been swept up in the huge burst of energy which rippled out from their great machine when it was activated for the very first time. But, in the process, the internal structure of the meteorite had itself been changed. The characteristics of my journey were written into it. Once they told me that, you can imagine the thought which came into my mind.'

'Did you try to get back to your monastery?' asked Awg.

'Of course. I was convinced that I had been shown another world for a purpose. I believed that I should return to pass on the news to my brethren. But I failed. It is probably just as well. What do you imagine would have happened to me if I had succeeded?'

'They'd have thought you were mad. Either that, or you'd have been burnt as a heretic.'

'Yes, that is what I think too. However, I did make my return to Llangarreg – but not in the manner I expected. Using the stone, I learnt to travel between the two worlds. But it was a perilous undertaking and I was pitifully unaware of the hazards. I was to learn some of them in my very first attempt.

'Gradually, I recognised where I was: it was the priory chapel – but it was in ruins. Of course, I had no idea what had happened. I did not know then about the destruction of the monasteries by King Henry. I could not have imagined an English king would do anything so wilful and so wicked. My dear home had been pulled down and I discovered it was now the year 1725. I was shocked and heartbroken but some stubbornness in me made me want to fight back. I made a vow that I would build something new from the ruins.'

'But what about the local people?' asked Awg. 'They must have been suspicious of someone suddenly popping up out of nowhere?'

'I was very lucky. I appeared at the time of the Shrovetide Fair in Pontrhyd and there were travellers everywhere. I said that I was on a pilgrimage to the old priory and no one thought it was out of the ordinary. The biggest problem was in learning the speech and customs of the day, so that I did not stand out as someone strange or threatening.'

Awg thought of his time in Gexadkydubm and being chased by the gang. He knew exactly how Benedict had felt.

'Fortunately,' continued the monk, ' I was usually able to make the excuse that I had led a sheltered life and knew little of the world. Most people either accepted that or took me for a simpleton.

'There was an old man in the village who made clocks, so I offered myself as his apprentice. I asked for no wages – only for bed and board and that I learned the trade. The old man found I was a willing and able pupil and I quickly became expert at my craft. When he died, I sent word to a few other brethren – for I had learned of places where my Order still survived. Together with helpers from nearby villages, we established the Llangarreg clockmakers' workshop.'

'But when did you make the black clock,' said Awg, 'and why did you put that spyridi thing inside it?'

'It was an act of vanity, for which I paid a terrible price. At that time, I made many journeys between the planet Zero and my workshop in Wales. On the last of them, I did a bad thing. My clocks had become famous for their craftsmanship and accuracy. I burned with a desire to make such a clock as had never been made before. It would keep perfect time and would run for ever. I stole a small power unit. Such a thing is common here, found in all manner of mechanical devices. Back in Llangarreg, I made a clock using every skill I knew, and to power and regulate it I used the spyridi cylinder. Then I sealed it up and put it on a shelf above my bench in our workshop. It was never intended that it should be sold or pass to anyone else. It was my masterpiece, made for my own satisfaction.

'But then fate took a hand. This time it was not the actions of a King that undid my life, but the very force of Nature itself. One night there was a terrible storm. Our workshop was struck by lightning and burnt to the ground. Everything I had built up was utterly destroyed.'

Forty Four

'I struggled up the path towards our workshop. The whole building was ablaze. But I had to get inside, to rescue the one thing I could not do without.'

'The black clock?' asked Awg.

'No,' replied Benedict. 'The stone. I kept it in a box under my workbench, where I thought it would be safe.

'I opened the door – and at first the heat and the smoke drove me back. But I was determined in my task and had no thought of danger or my own safety.

'I got to my bench and snatched up the box, but it was already badly burned and the stone fell through the bottom and rolled across the floor. I rushed to pick it up and ...'

He broke off and shuddered, as if in pain. Then the monk pulled up the sleeves of his habit so that Awg could see his arms.

It was Awg's turn to wince as he saw the livid blotches and ugly scars.

'The fire was all about me. As my hands closed around the scalding stone, I sensed that I was no longer master of my destiny. Perhaps some memory of its own fiery descent from the heavens was stirring within the stone itself. The last thing I remember is the flames around me getting fainter and fainter and then dissolving away completely.

'When I at last awoke, I was back in this house. Zwnerbas had cared for me and healed my wounds, and the spyridi had saved for me the remains of my stone. It had fractured in the heat and was crumbling to powder. They told me that the action of the atmosphere would soon have destroyed it completely, and so they hit upon a beautiful way to preserve what was left. Would you like to see it?'

Awg nodded.

Benedict went to a cupboard. 'Here is my meteorite.'

'Where?' gasped Awg.

Benedict held up the hourglass.

'It is no ordinary sand you see inside. It is the meteorite. The spyridi sealed it up within this glass. All the air has been pumped out so that what remains is safe.'

'And it must still have its power,' said Awg. 'Otherwise, how could we have met in the chapel?'

'You are right. For many years I thought that its properties had been destroyed. Then a chance event showed me that this was not true, and I returned to Llangarreg. But, once again, centuries had passed. The fire was now but a distant memory and I found myself in the Earthworld of your own day. I travel from time to time, to remind myself of the noble mountains and green valleys. Especially, to hear the sound of running water …'

Benedict lapsed into silence.

'But – I am allowing myself to forget why you have come.' He rose and beckoned Awg to follow.

'I must fulfil my promise to the spyridi and show you the answer to your own question.'

Benedict led the way back to the building in which Awg had first met Xurog. They did not go inside but walked around to a long, low-roofed structure at the rear. Two black pyramidal columns guarded the entrance. It was quite dark inside and their footsteps echoed on the stone floor. When Awg's eyes had become accustomed to the dimness, he saw that the walls were covered in stone tablets carrying hieroglyphic inscriptions. Set into each stone was a circle of black glass. Awg went up to one and stared inside. He was startled to see a 3-dimensional picture of a zwnerba. He looked in more of the windows. In every one were similar images: some of zwnerbas, some of Zeroian humanoids, some of spyridi – and some of beings that he did not recognise.

'Who are they?' he asked, in a hushed voice.

'They are the pioneers who were lost. This is the Hall of Memory. It is dedicated to all those who have perished in the exploration of Space. Over there are plaques to early astronauts who died in accidents to their spacecraft. In that central section are casualties of the plasma transfer process.'

He took Awg over to the tablets on the end wall of the building.

'Here are the Adventurers. It is their memorials which I brought you here to see. I bow my head in their presence, for I myself am responsible for their deaths.'

Awg was deeply shocked. How could this kindly man have killed anyone? It was impossible. After a few moments silence, Benedict continued:

'Xurog has told you that my unexpected appearance alerted the scientists of the day to the existence of the Dark Universe. They were excited to learn of the planet Earth and resolved to see it for themselves. But how could they find something that was invisible? The plasma transport process provided the only link. They first tried to use the meteorite in the simple way that I did, but the attempt failed completely. So then they made a determined effort to decode the structural changes discovered within the stone – and they used this as the basis for programming their machine.

'An expedition was organised and a group of volunteer Adventurers sent out on a trajectory towards the Earth. They were lost without trace. Nevertheless, two further attempts were made, at each stage refining the location information to increase the chance of success – but to no avail. All we know is that the explorers left here. They have never re-appeared anywhere within our domain. Where they went, and where they are now in time and space, is unknown. It seems certain to me that they perished, long ago.'

Benedict raised his arms towards the walls, where the memorial tablets looked down on them, rank upon rank.

'These are monuments to brave people – but they are also

reminders to us of our ignorance. There is so much that even the Spyridi themselves do not understand. How can beings from Earth live here on Zero? How is it that the peoples from the two worlds can see each other? Why is it that I alone have been able to make the return journey?' Did my own body become physically changed, like the stone itself? Perhaps that is why I have lived so long!'

He turned to Awg.

'So you see, what Xurog wishes you to understand is this. It is not that they do not want you to return, or seek to prevent it – it is that they do not know how such a thing can be accomplished. It is beyond the limit of their knowledge.'

*

Awg walked back to his room in sombre mood. It seemed to him quite possible that the Adventurers from Zero *had* reached the Earth. There were enough strange tales to account for it. Benedict didn't realise how lucky he'd been. He hadn't got immediately hacked to death. His captors had been prepared to persevere until some understanding was gained. In turn, they had themselves benefited from Benedict's wisdom.

He thought bitterly of all the sci-fi films he'd seen. Killer aliens, Martians with death rays, Things from Outer Space: all monsters, and all wanting to take over the Earth. He'd zapped a good few himself in computer games. He knew all too well what would happen if giant spider-like beings and huge, grey-skinned zwnerbas suddenly appeared in Trafalgar Square, or even in Strenton market. Human beings would find it difficult to appreciate the arrival of unusual visitors whose only motive was peaceful curiosity.

Forty Five

Next morning, Awg found Zert waiting for him outside. In silence, they walked across the green.

'There's worse places,' said Zert, eventually. 'What about you'd got stuck on Hano? The surface's so hot they gotta live on platforms built over the lava pools. Best thing you'd see all day's ten miles o' boilin' mud going glurp glurp.'

'Perhaps that's where those explorers went, poor sods,' replied Awg miserably. 'Thought they were going to Earth and ended up in the lava pools.'

'Nope. If they was there, we'd know. Anywhere in our Universe we got contact. Light beams, radio waves, all that stuff. But it don't work for your world. None of it gets here, or if it does we can't detect it. Nope, either they got to your Universe or they're still suspended.'

'Suspended?' queried Awg.

'In transit – dispersed from one place but not materialised in another yet.'

'Like on a train stuck outside a station waiting to get onto a platform?'

'Dunno 'bout that, but it sounds the right idea.'

'So they might appear anywhere, at any time?'

'Could do. Might even end up on your Earth after all. Like I told you, plasma transport's tricky.'

Awg thought about his own journey – and how that had turned out.

'Zert, what happens if – if your body's not prepared for the process and goes into shock?'

'It's not a problem for spyridi, we're always OK. But with your sort o' body, it can really screw things up. You gotta get treated pretty quick.'

'And if you're not?'

'The cell chemistry goes bananas – which means you dies.'

It took Awg a few moments for the force of this to sink in. He'd been thinking of Asa as saving him from five years three months and ten days in prison. Now it seemed as if, without her, he wouldn't have even got to start his sentence. Awg suddenly wanted to see her again, very badly.

'When's Asa coming back?'

'Expectin' her today,' answered Zert. 'Alert at Chykideyh's over. No more intruders found. Nothin' robbed or trashed. Whole thing's totally weird.

'Seems Asa's bringin' the guy they found back here. Dunno why. Hope she knows what she's doin' – could be dangerous.'

They had reached a tall rectangular building with an array of antennae on its roof.

'This is it,' said Zert. 'I promised I'd show you some stuff 'bout the beacons.'

They went inside and Zert took Awg along to a cylindrical lift. It was frighteningly like those in Tukzadryk and the old fort, and Awg felt very uncomfortable. They went far down into the depths of the building. Zert led them into a huge room. Spyridi, zwnerbas and a few Zeroians were working at the rows of desks and consoles which filled the space. Zert took his place at a vacant desk and began to manipulate the controls with astonishing speed.

'Whaddya want to find out, then? Current wind speeds in the atmosphere o' Ospiros? That's the planet the spyridi come from origin'ly. I never been there, though.

'What 'bout a temperature profile through the core o' the biggest volcano on Hano?' Zert flicked rapidly through a series of graphs and charts. Then he paused.

'Tha's all real time stuff. Standard technology. Let's go up the wow-scale a bit. Somethin' different. What 'bout this?'

The black cube began to glow and, slowly, an image formed on each of its faces. Awg watched in wonder. First, a pattern of seemingly random dots; then the dots became clusters; and then, at each scan of the screen, more detail appeared, until a definite picture was visible. Not a picture like those on TV. More the outlines of things, like a pencil sketch an artist might do in a few minutes. But then Awg recognised what it was. He craned his neck from one side to the other, comparing the pictures on the cube faces.

'I just can't believe I'm seeing this,' he whispered. 'It's the view from Gellyn mountain. In all directions.'

'Yep. It's the nearest beacon to where your transfer started. It's the one Garik always wants to look at.'

Awg whistled. So his gran had been right. In a way, someone had been watching them when they were on the mountain. But it wasn't the monks. He made a mental note to be very careful of any large white rocks he sat on in the future.

'So is that picture ... live?' he asked. 'Like, what's there at this very moment?'

Zert clicked, and wobbled his head from one side to the other.

'Yes an' no. You gotta remember the way that picture's made. From huge computer calcs based on tiny changes 'round that beacon – like the light an' shade fallin' on it in different directions. That's Xurog's proximity effect I told you 'bout. So it's built up mighty gradually, an' it's still buildin' now. It's like an average view over a long time.'

'But how does it get here?' said Awg, scratching his head. 'You said that the one Universe can't see the other.'

'That's the clever bit. The electromagnetic radiation from each world is invis'ble to the other – that's light an' radio waves an' stuff, like I said before – but each feels the other's gravity. Now the effect o' gravity can work like a wave, so what Xurog did was to find a way o' transmittin' information usin' gravity as the carrier wave, jus' like you can do with radio signals on radio waves. The difference is, the gravity signals interact with both *our* Universe *an'* the Dark World an' can pass from one to the other. I told you Xurog was a genius.'

Zert swayed from side to side, obviously very pleased with himself.

'Now,' he said. 'D'you wanna see where Asa is? They took off two hours ago an' I bin trackin' their progress.'

'Those helicars do have a navigation system, then?'

'Nah. They got a crude autopilot an' that's it. But Asa's got her own locator module an' we can track that. I'll show you.'

The picture on the front screen dissolved. In its place appeared a 3-D map of the country outside.

'There's the receivin' station at Chykideyh,' said Zert, 'an' here's the portal for Auyvhasdh – an' here's Asa.'

He pointed to a red line being projected on the map. It started at Chykideyh and went across the map about half way to Auyvhasdh. They sat and watched.

'Why isn't it moving?' said Awg. 'Or haven't I understood it properly?'

'It *is* movin',' said Zert. 'Jus' watch – the line's gettin' longer.'

They watched for several minutes. The line didn't get any longer.

'Perhaps it isn't working,' suggested Awg.

Zert clicked in annoyance. Spyridi technology didn't go wrong, or at least not very often. He moved a small disc rapidly across the surface of a graduated silver sphere.

'That's coded a call message to her communicator. Now she'll respond to confirm her speed an' position.'

They waited.

There was no answer.

Forty Six

Awg hurried over to the transit station to watch the rescue preparations. Everything was being kept as low key as possible. There might be a simple explanation for the loss of contact with Asa. It was vital that no word got out that the Patrician's daughter could be missing, either to her friends – or to her enemies. There was no knowing what either group might do in such a crisis.

Zert was there too. His friends back at the monitoring centre were keeping a continuous scan on all the channels that might carry any message from Asa. So far, there had been nothing.

Together, Awg and Zert watched the fuelling of the transporter. Xurog had ordered Berjga to bring in the best vehicle available and it was there in a far corner of the station being charged up with hydrogen. They watched the armed zwnerba guards load their kit into the plane. Part of a commando unit trained in search and rescue, they had been flown in on Xurog's orders from one of the desert bases.

'What's it like where the red line ended on the map?' asked Awg. He pictured Asa's plane stranded in the sort of rough grassland he'd so often seen in his travels. Not too bad for an emergency landing – and you'd be easily spotted from the air.

'The Stone Forest,' said Zert. 'Weird area. It's desert, with towers o' rock scattered all over. Nowhere much for a transporter to land if it was in trouble.'

The fuel lines were disconnected and final preparations made. For a moment, everything was quiet. The doors of the helicar had been left wide open. Awg looked at Zert, who glanced back and nodded. They checked that none of the warning globes was showing a blue light and then stepped over the boundary wire and crept across to the transporter.

Inside, the door to the small cargo bay was open. Very little had been loaded into it. There wasn't a lot of room inside, but ...

Awg remembered what spiders did on Earth when cornered.

'Zert,' he asked casually. 'Can you squeeze yourself down really small, like into a ball?'

They both looked at the cargo bay. Zert shook his head.

'Don' even *think* 'bout it,' he said. 'This is Xurog's show. There's a lot ridin' on its success. If we was to louse it up ... ' He shuddered. 'I only seen Xurog really mad once, an' it was scary. Besides, this is *dangerous*. Even if she's just crashed in bad weather, it'll be tough enough to find her – but p'raps there's more to it than that. There's people that don't 'xactly wish her a long an' happy life.'

'Such as?'

'You've met Sharibvdl – an' seen what he's like. There's others in the shadows that's a lot worse.'

'Even more reason, then,' said Awg. 'I've just got to go. She rescued me from prison and got me across the desert. If she's in trouble, I've got to help. I don't mind going on my own.'

'That's crazy. There's stuff on this planet you can't even imagine. You'll need help.'

The globe next to the transporter lit up orange. A door in the nearest building opened.

Awg and Zert exchanged glances.

'OK, let's do it,' said Zert.

And in a moment they were aboard, into the cargo bay and sliding its door across. Awg left it a crack open, so that he could *just* see out.

The crew got in. Awg hoped fervently that each of them would think the other had closed the door. He pressed his eye to the crack. First aboard was Berjga, who strapped herself into the pilot's seat. Next came the two zwnerba guards, who occupied the passenger seats, one beside the pilot and one behind.

A blue glare shone into the plane. Awg couldn't see the warning globe outside but guessed that the transit procedure had been initiated. The process was less frightening inside the dark confines of the cargo space because you weren't so aware of the visual effects. Awg got a glimpse of their multiple reflections vanishing into the void and then came the blinding light of their exit from the black pyramid. Berjga taxied around the space for a few minutes, presumably to get used to being out in the normal world again, and then took off.

If the helicars had seemed noisy when Awg had been sitting comfortably in the cabin, that was nothing to the din inside the cargo bay. The level of sound was deafening, and every possible joint and hinge shook and rattled as if about to disintegrate.

'We're flyin' north,' whispered Zert.

'You've got a compass?' hissed Awg.

'No, spyridi don' need one. We can tell.'

The space inside the cargo bay was extremely cramped. Squashing up against Zert was an unnerving experience, rather like sharing the space with a very large pineapple or cactus: very knobbly and prickly. Awg didn't let his mind dwell on the fact that the prickles and knobbles were the hairs and joints on the legs of a curled up three foot spider-being.

The box that the zwnerba guards had stowed in the cargo bay was sticking painfully into his back. He manoeuvred it around until it was underneath him and then perched himself on top of it. He didn't want to damage any of the rescue equipment but the box seemed strong and solid enough. It ought to be OK to sit on it.

The box had a dial on the front that Awg assumed was some sort of combination lock. In the darkness he could not see that the numbers on the row of four wheels were slowly changing. At the moment they said 0629*. A little later they said 0617.

They flew on for about an hour and a half and then seemed

* What they actually said looked something like ждΨш. Translation from Zeroian into the base-10 system with arabic numerals gives 0629.

to hit a patch of turbulence. Awg felt two distinct lurches in the motion of the plane but then things seemed to settle down again and they flew on steadily. In the cargo hold, the row of wheels on the box had reached 0018.

'I hope they've got all the right kit to help them with the rescue,' whispered Awg.

'Bound to,' breathed Zert. 'Xurog said they was from a crack team, spec'lly trained for this sort o' stuff.'

'But wouldn't you expect they'd bring loads of ropes and stretchers and medical things? There's only the box that's in here and the stuff they've got in their backpacks. I wonder why they didn't put those in the hold as well? They can't be very comfortable with them on.'

'You mean they didn' take 'em off, even when they got to their seats?'

'No, I watched them strap themselves in, backpacks and all.'

Zert suddenly unwound and pushed Awg to one side. Awg nearly fell off the box. He stifled a cry of pain as his shoulder slammed into the bulkhead, not wanting to give their presence away. Zert peered through the gap into the cabin.

A second later, he let out a roar and flung back the door. There was no one in the pilot's seat. Berjga was lying in a crumpled heap on the floor. The passenger seats were empty.

In the cargo hold, the row of wheels on the box had reached 0006.

Forty Seven

'They've bailed out!' shouted Zert. 'Those backpacks was parachutes. They've gone!'

Awg rushed over to Berjga. She seemed completely lifeless and there was an ugly yellow patch on the grey skin of her neck. He looked ahead to see where they were flying, terrified that the pilotless plane would be hurtling into a mountainside. But they were locked on to a steady course and the airspace ahead of them was clear.

'They left the box,' said Awg. 'Why did they leave the box?'

They both knew.

They dragged it out of the cargo hold. The dial on the front said 0002.

They tore open the loading hatch and, between them, swung the box out. For a few moments they watched it drop away from them.

'Shut the hatch an' grab on to somethin'!' shouted Zert.

The hatch slammed shut and they both sank to the floor holding on to the passenger seats.

The box had reached about half way to the valley floor when it ceased to be a box. It became a ball of fire, expanding and expanding; then a miss-shapen ball, as flaming chunks of its ugly heart plummeted to the ground.

Then the shock wave hit the plane, punching it upwards and sideways. Awg and Zert were thrown across the cabin and the transporter went into a nosedive.

'Can you fly one of these things?' Awg screamed to Zert.

'Nope! Can you?'

Awg scrambled over to the controls and racked his brains to remember what he had seen when he flew with Asa. He strapped himself into the pilot's seat. It would be rough going.

'I gotta keep my head … I gotta keep my head …' The words went round and round in his brain like a tape loop.

And at the back of his mind some demon was chanting the chorus, 'Or you're gonna be dead, you're gonna be dead …'

One. Unlock the autopilot. Get control back.

Two. The lever in the centre altered the thrust from the main rotor. Notch it up to increase the pitch and bring the plane out of its dive. More, more.

Three. The central grip regulated the engine speed. Rack it up, up, up. Got to straighten out and climb.

Four. The handles at each side altered the angle of the rotor blades to govern the direction of flight. Steady, steady. Keep – them – steady. Yes. *Yes.*

Somehow, he got control.

He was breathing so hard now he thought his chest would burst. Sweat flooded down his face. Zert crouched low in the passenger seat.

Awg knew he'd got to get the plane down. Otherwise, he'd be bound to hit something sooner or later, or at best keep the thing in the air until it ran out of fuel and they crashed anyway.

They were flying over a strange desert landscape. Awg recognised it at once from Zert's description of the Stone Forest. Blocks and towers of rock reared up from the valley floor, striped and striated with bands of different colours – every shade of yellow, red and brown. Some were huge mesas, with flat tops the size of football pitches; others were narrow and pointed: the remains of a sandstone plateau, weathered down by desert storms until only its bones remained.

He headed for the largest of the stone towers. The top was enormous and looked fairly flat. He managed to slow down as he approached, gradually reducing his height. They were about to pass over the upper lip of the mesa when they ran into the updraft from the valley floor. The transporter bucked and swayed. Awg fought the controls and steadied out. He dropped the engine speed and flattened the rotors. Now they were about half way across the top and slowing, slowing ... drifting ... now almost hovering.

How did you land? He'd never really noticed. He'd been too busy goggling at the giant black pyramid as they approached Auyvhasdh.

He notched down the engine and reduced the thrust ... more, more, more ...

And suddenly they were on the deck, bumping and bouncing, slewing from side to side ... approaching the other side of the mesa. The land dropped away shear for perhaps a thousand feet.

Brakes. The thing had to have brakes. It went on roads too. There was a single round pedal on the floor. Awg stamped on it and they squealed to a stop, about 50 yards from the far edge of the mesa.

'You done it. You done it. *You actually done it!*' Zert was capering about in an ecstasy of relief.

Awg didn't hear him. A warm, dark blanket of unconsciousness was rolling towards him and, utterly exhausted, he wrapped himself gratefully inside it.

As he drifted away, a crazy message trickled through his head, like the one he'd imagined a long time before, way back in the gardens of the Patrician's palace, in the city of Gexadkydubm:

Dear Mum

Lots of things have happened since I wrote last time. I did get to see the King person but he was sad. Actually, he would have been a lot more upset if he'd realised his daughter was a freedom fighter. I'm not to call her a Princess or she'll break my arm. We left the first city and went to another one. We got sucked into a giant pyramid but it's all OK because the spiders are in control. I shan't be home for a while because I'm in a different Universe. You can't see it through a telescope because it's invisible. I met the monk I saw in Llangarreg but he doesn't get out much on account of being nearly a thousand years old. There's a bit of trouble here at the moment but if we can find Asa there probably won't be a war. I flew a plane today and luckily managed to land on a big rock a thousand feet above the desert. It was a good job we threw the bomb out because it went off a few seconds later and I'd been sitting on it for about two hours. I've only managed to wash once so far because of the water shortage but a kind alien cleaned my clothes so it's all right.

Love
Allardyce

Forty Eight

Awg was warm and relaxed.

'Wake up. Wake up. You just gotta wake up!'

Awg didn't want to wake up, but Zert shook him until he did.

Straightaway, they checked on Berjga. She was breathing but showed no sign of regaining consciousness.

'I guess they got her from behind with a stun gun,' said Zert. 'That'd account for that yellow welt on her neck.'

They made her as comfortable as they could in the cramped confines of the cabin. At least they had shelter. Outside, the wind had got up and was whipping the dust into yellow swirls around their craft.

They searched the cabin for anything that might be useful and found some food and water that Berjga had brought with her. That would keep them going for a bit. They found Berjga's communicator under one of the seats. It had been smashed to pieces. Components and wires lay about the floor.

'Lucky I got mine, then,' said Zert.

'You've got a radio?'

'Lot more'n a radio – it's a project I bin workin' on. Got some other stuff too. Show you in a minute.'

'How come you've got all these things?' asked Awg.

'Told you in Gexadkydubm. I'm a trainee. If you're gonna qualify as a full technician, you gotta do projects, invent things. I always got stuff on me.

'Now I gotta try an' get through to Auyvhasdh without alertin' Xurog. Gonna be difficult. Big encryption job.'

He worked on the communicator for several minutes and then came back to Awg.

'I called the monitor centre first, 'cos I got friends there I can trust. There's still been nothin' from Asa an' now they're panickin' 'cos they've lost contact with Berjga as well.'

'Well, we know …' began Awg.

'Listen! Their plan was, as soon as she reported a definite sightin' of Asa or her plane, more transporters with full equipment would be sent out as back-up. Apparently that's now bin cancelled on the direct orders o' Xurog.'

'Which means?'

'Which means either he's got a new plan, or … I don't wanna think 'bout the "or" 'cos it'd mean he was expectin' the news on Berjga. If that's true, we're all finished.'

'I don't believe Xurog's a traitor,' said Awg. 'If he wanted to get Asa he must've had dozens of opportunities already. And he hasn't.'

Zert snorted. 'Unless he's bin waitin' for a chance like this to get things started – playin' the good guy all the time an' then just *havin'* to move in an' take control himself.'

'So did you tell your friends the truth – about what happened and where we are?'

'Yep,' said Zert. 'An' they're keepin' it to themselves. So anythin' can happen now. We're on our own.'

They were startled by a noise behind them. They turned to see Berjga sitting up. She looked awful. She rocked herself to and fro and then vomited. They sat with her, gave her water and a little food, and told her what had happened.

At first she refused to believe that Awg had landed the plane on his own. 'The people from your planet must be very clever,' she said, eventually.

'No, not clever at all,' said Awg emphatically. 'I was just very, very lucky.'

It was agreed that the first and most important task was to resume their original mission and find Asa. Zert tuned his communicator in to the monitor room in Auyvhasdh and got a fix on the exact position where contact had been lost. They were only a few miles from the spot.

While they were waiting for Berjga to recover, Zert produced a roll of rubbery film and went outside. He covered the whole of the helicar dome with the material. From the outside, the dome was no longer transparent but appeared a dull silver-grey. However, from the inside, the coating was invisible and they could see out as clearly as before.

'What's it for?' asked Awg.

'Protection,' said Zert, simply.

'Does it keep bullets off, then?'

'Nope. Don't need to. Nobody's used stuff like that for years.'

'So, what does it do?'

''nother project. Theory is, some light gets through but other radiation's reflected. Come in handy if we're attacked with a laser weapon or somethin.'

'The *theory*?'

'Like I said, it's a project. Might not work. Needs testin.'

Awg had a very uneasy feeling about this.

When Berjga felt well enough, they took off again and set a course for Asa's last reported position. The search took them north-east, where the desert gave way to an arid scrubland dotted with spiny, blue-grey bushes. The rock towers became lower and rounder, sometimes with scraps of ragged woodland on their tops. It was on one of these that they found the wreckage of Asa's transporter. It had hit the trees on the side of the hill and broken in two. The transparent dome and most of the cabin were lodged in a tree and the wheeled undercarriage was lying upside down about twenty yards away, where some of the hillside was blackened and smouldering. There was no sign of anyone about.

They made several circuits of the hill, circling lower each time, trying to get a more detailed view.

'Look – over there!' Awg had spotted some movement lower down the hillside. As they descended, they could see where an overhanging cliff provided some shelter. On the ledge beneath stood a figure, waving its arms. But it was not Asa. It was no one that any of them had ever seen before. As they flew lower, they could make out the details. It was definitely not one of the spyridi (incorrect shape and number of limbs) and certainly not a zwnerba (not tall enough, wrong colour, incorrect number of eyes). Only Awg knew – suddenly, instinctively and impossibly – who it was. It might have been a native Zeroian, although that was unlikely. Few Zeroians had white hair, or dressed in tweed jackets and grey flannel trousers.

Forty Nine

There was nowhere to land on the steep hillside near the crashed plane.

They were still circling when the first rocket shell took off their rear nearside wheel. Two transporters were closing in on them.

'This ain't possible,' said Zert. 'Transporters don't carry arms.'

They saw the streak of the second rocket shell, and waited for the impact. The plane lurched and shook but there was no explosion. A black oily substance began to pour out underneath them. Berjga banked sharply and began to climb. They could see the two remaining rockets mounted at the side of the helicar that was firing on them. Any moment now ...

Zert ripped out his communicator and pointed it at the attacking transporter. He worked feverishly at the controls, struggling to lock on. After a few seconds of bleeps, the set gave out a long, continuous high note.

'OKaayyyyyy!' he said, deftly keying in the codes he'd located. 'Now we wait for 'em to fire again.'

'I don't mind waiting for quite a long time,' said Awg, who was flat on the floor.

Their attacker banked around the hillside, then levelled with them. Berjga dived, but so did the other plane. As they pulled out, there was a flash from the side of the armed helicar and Awg braced himself for the hit. But no rocket came screaming towards them. Instead, the attacking transporter lurched into a spin and seemed to be on fire. Seconds later, it exploded in a blaze of flame and plummeted to the valley floor.

Zert gave a crow of triumph. But the second helicar now began closing in. The rockets on the fallen transporter had been obvious. This second one was different. There were no guns each side but underneath the nose of the dome was a squat black cylinder. Awg didn't like the look of it at all. From the sudden tensing of eight limbs, Awg guessed that Zert didn't like the look of it much either.

'Forbidden weapon,' he said. 'No one's allowed these. Production was outlawed years ago.'

'What is it?' whispered Awg.

'Plasma cannon. Only seen pictures o' them. Great test for my reflector, though. If it works, I'll write it up. Certain to get top marks.'

'And if it doesn't?' asked Awg, suspecting he already knew the answer.

'Then it won't matter what marks any o' us would've got.'

The second transporter climbed sharply and then dived straight towards them. A green glare lit up the whole cabin. Awg froze and closed his eyes. He had a bad feeling that this was it. There was going to be no one left to rescue Asa.

The glare faded.

Awg raised his head off the floor and looked towards the attacking plane. It wasn't there. Seconds later, a large black dot appeared in the sky about half a mile away. It careened into the side of a mountain and burst into a thousand smoking fragments.

'That was goin' to be us,' said Zert. 'Those cannons – they're locality-shifters. They was used in wars years ago. You locks on to a target, picks a point where you wants the target shifted to – an' energise the beam. They don' need much energy 'cos what you uses for the dispersion you gets back from the materialisation. So you can gettem real small an' put 'em in vehicles.'

He waved several of his arms in the air. 'Warn't the reflector brilliant! I'll get an A* for that.'

Awg was glad it hadn't turned out to be a D "must try harder".

'And what did you do to the rocket?' asked Berjga.

'Locked on an' scrambled the firin' sequence. Shell couldn't leave its harness an' ignited where it was. Luck'ly, got hot 'nough to detonate. By the way, what happened to that second rocket?'

Beneath them, black oil still dripped from the undercarriage, where a large cylindrical object sat jammed in a mass of broken pipework.

Fifty

It wasn't easy to land the transporter with one wheel missing and none of the hydraulics working, but Berjga got them down safely.

The rocky hill on which Asa had crashed rose out of the scrubland in the form of a lopsided letter 'M'. Its flanks were steep and crumbling and a wide rift ran down the centre. Berjga had managed to land on the larger side of the rift, where the hillocky mass of gravel and sand provided a few relatively flat areas. The remains of Asa's plane lay beyond the gulf on the far side of the hill. Below the wreckage, the ground fell away steeply in a confusion of stunted trees, scree and boulders.

Zert got on to his friends in Auyvhasdh and reported the finding of Asa's plane. He knew that further action was desperately needed – but what could they do? The only person with the authority to send help was Xurog. Zert was also uneasy about their attackers – had they sent for reinforcements before they got blown to bits?

They left the helicar and walked as far as the canyon rim. Awg looked at the yawning gulf. Somehow they'd got to get across. They must find out about Asa. If she was alive, they had to get her to safety. If she wasn't, then they were probably all doomed anyway.

'Haven't we got a rope or *something*?' said Awg in desperation.

Berjga jumped up. 'The transporter has a winch – under the floor,' she said. 'When we drive in the desert, we need the winch to pull the car back if it goes off the road.'

To get to the winch drum they had to open the undercarriage

of the helicar. It was then that they discovered the shell. They also discovered how fast one of the spyridi could run. By the time Awg and Berjga had caught up and joined Zert behind a large rock, he was feeling a bit ashamed of himself.

'Sorry 'bout that,' he said. 'Warn't thinkin' too logic'ly. Didn't go boom when it hit us an' it's sat there for a couple o' hours – so why should it go off now?'

Awg decided he'd wait for a very good reason before going back.

Zert explained. 'Shells like that ain't usually time-fused. They're designed to detonate on impact – an' it didn't. Luckily.'

'I got an idea,' he added. 'Just goin' to have 'nother look.'

Awg and Berjga got up to follow him but he pushed them back.

'Wait a bit – just in case.'

'In case of what?' said Awg, remembering that Zert had said that transporters never carried arms. Just before they were fired on.

'Just in case,' said Zert.

In a few minutes, they heard a shout. 'It's OK. Youc'n come. It's safe.'

To their horror, he had dragged the rocket out and laid it on the ground.

'It's in three sections. The back bit's th'ignition stage, an' that's burnt up. The middle's the propellant, an' only a part of that's fired.'

'And the front bit?' asked Awg.

'That's th'explosive charge. I gotta get that off. Either it's a dud or the impact warn't big enough on account o' the rocket not firin' prop'ly. It should be OK. They're not usually booby-trapped. Just gimme an hour or two.'

Awg and Berjga looked at one another in a way that said, "Do we let him do this?"

'D'you have any other suggestions?' responded Zert. 'Trust me. I'm good at stuff like this.'

Berjga and Awg went and sat at the top of a small hill – a

considerable distance away. They jumped at every noise they heard, terrified of being bombarded with bits of the transporter – and Zert.

Two hours later, they met together at the canyon. Zert showed them what he had done. The bits of the unexploded missile and the winch from the transporter had both been put to good use.

'Here's the rocket section. I cleaned out the burnt stuff, so it should go. Had to improvise on the ignition side, so that's dodgy. It fires up by remote – I made that from bits o' Berjga's communicator. The back's fastened to the winch cable an' the axle of the drum's wedged between those rocks. I've aimed the rocket at that sandy cliff at the top on the far side. With a bit o' luck it'll go a fair way in an' get stuck.'

Berjga was amazed. 'Do you seriously think this can work?' she asked.

'It's all we got,' replied Zert. 'So we gotta give it a go. I think p'raps we'd better get back a bit, just in case things don't go quite right.'

They cowered behind the largest rock they could find.

Zert got out his communicator.

'You ready?'

They nodded.

Zert pressed the button.

Nothing happened.

Awg could hear a spluttering sound. He stuck his head around the side of the rock. Smoke was pouring out of the back of the rocket from Zert's makeshift ignition pack. Then there was a spurt of flame. Awg ducked back just in time.

With a roar that echoed up and down the canyon, the rocket hurtled across the space and whacked into the bank on the other side with a sound like a traffic accident. Awg looked up to see the wire hawser streaking across the gap, the coils unravelling like a maddened snake. The impetus wrenched the drum out from behind the rock and into the air. They watched with dismay as it headed towards the gulf – and crashed to earth just a few feet from the drop. Even then, the weight of the swinging cable jerked it further and further towards the edge. Awg was sure it was going over. All Zert's work ruined and their only hope gone.

Then it stopped, pulled up by the length of wire Zert had fixed to its base, the other end hammered into the ground with a bolt he'd robbed from the winch.

'Lucky 'bout that,' said Zert. 'Jus' thought it might be needed.'

Awg stood staring at the smoking hole on the opposite side where the far end of the cable was now anchored. He couldn't believe it had worked.

'What did you make the fuse out of?' he asked, in a shocked voice.

'Cut up a bit o' the high explosive from the front end,' said Zert. 'Just burns if you don't confine it.

''Course, I had to find a way to get the detonator out first,' he added.

Fifty One

They wound the cable taut, gingerly at first, praying that the other end wouldn't pull out from the opposite bank. It seemed secure.

'We gotta make sure,' said Zert. 'If it's gonna go, it better go now 'fore anyone gets on it.'

All three of them threw their weight against the winch drum. The line held fast. Zert locked the drum in place and bolted it to the ground.

Someone was going to have to get over the other side. It seemed to Awg there was an obvious choice. He himself wasn't all that keen. And if you were roughly the shape of a giraffe, climbing across canyons on wires didn't seem a particularly good idea. On the other hand, if you were agile and compact – and especially if you had eight arms ...

Zert knew they were looking at him.

'OK you guys,' he said. 'There's somethin' I gotta tell you. I'm good at fixin' stuff an' all that, but' – he looked desperately uncomfortable – 'I'm scared o' heights!'

He noted the stares of disbelief.

'I know, I know! But it's true. You're gonna have to count me out on this one.'

Any further discussion was cut short by a cry from the opposite side of the canyon. The man in the tweed jacket was shouting at them and waving his arms about. He was pointing over the hill in the direction of Asa's crashed transporter. They couldn't hear what he was saying but they got the message. Where there had previously been a few grey whisps from the smouldering wreck site, a thick blue smoke was now belching into the air. It looked as if the whole hillside could be on fire.

Someone had to get across and Awg knew it was now up to him. He looked at the wire, stretched taut above the chasm. The obvious way would be to go across underneath, monkey-fashion, winding your legs around the cable and using your hands to get along. Somehow, he didn't fancy it.

He looked across the ravine. About 30 yards. The same distance as the wall above Nicholson's jam factory, although the drop was greater. Two hundred feet greater.

Awg took his trainers off and knotted them around his neck with the laces. He had made up his mind. For the second time in his life, he felt that he could do it.

He stood up on the drum, then stepped out on to the cable. He felt the wire beneath his toes. Here, at its anchor point, it was very firm and solid. Awg knew that further out things would be very different. He tried swaying from side to side and found he could retain his balance. He took a few cautious steps until he was at the place where the cable ran out over the edge. This was the last point at which he could stop. Until he was at the other side.

He took a quick look down. The sides of the ravine dropped away in a rampart of rough yellow rock to where, ages ago, a river had cascaded through the gorge. From this height, the parched rocks in its dry bed looked no larger than grains of sand. It was unreal, like a model. If anyone fell, you'd hardly see them. There would just be another grain of sand, redder than the rest. If anyone fell ...

Awg raised his arms from his sides and stretched them out. Then, looking straight ahead, he stepped out on to the wire.

Over nothing.

Although he could not see them, three people were standing absolutely still, unable to believe their eyes. They had become statues.

After a few steps, the solid feel of the wire began to evaporate. It started to become elastic. At every step he took, the bounce increased. It was like walking on a springy mattress. A one-inch wide springy mattress. But he kept on going.

As he approached the half-way point, the cable began to sway. It was getting much harder to keep his balance. Awg's eyes were riveted on his target on the far side of the gulf. He resisted any temptation to look from side to side or (much worse) down. So he didn't see the patch of grease that had rubbed off from the drum.

He went steadily forward. One step. Then another. Then another. It was vital to keep that regular rhythm. One step. One step. One step.

He became aware of something glistening just ahead of him. Awg thought how odd it was that the cable should be wet. It never rained on Zero, or at least not when he'd been around. And then he realised what it was.

He forced his eyes lower and allowed them to focus on the wire. No further. *He must not look down.* He judged the distance between him and the grease. Slowly, he raised his gaze back to his target at the opposite edge. Two small steps. One large step. The blob of grease was behind him.

But he had broken his rhythm and the wire swayed wildly. He fought to keep his balance, his arms windmilling around. One step. One step. One step. One step.

It was harder now because the natural slope of the cable was against him. He was going uphill; only slightly, but his feet were trying to slip back. He curled his toes around the wire and kept going. He was getting tired and the muscles of his legs ached like hell. One step. One step. One step. One step.

He was nearly there when suddenly the wire shook and an avalanche of small stones rattled down the rock face in front of him. Awg froze. Was the cable starting to pull out? Or was it just settling as Awg's weight drew closer and forced it down against the lip of the shell-hole? Awg waited a very long half-minute, but there was no further movement. With a huge effort, he struggled forward to the end of the cable and collapsed against the cliff.

What had not been apparent from his starting point was that the rocket had embedded itself some way below the top of the precipice. It had looked such a short distance from the other side but from close up it was different. Awg was now balancing on a wire, 200 feet above the floor of the canyon and eight feet from its top. The rock was a crumbly sandstone and impossible to climb. So how was he going to get up?

He looked back towards Zert and Berjga, hoping for inspiration. To his horror, he saw that something was crawling along the cable towards him. Trapped at the end of the wire, he had no way of escaping it, whatever it was. At first, he thought it was a large insect. Was it poisonous? Then he could see that it was disc-shaped and didn't seem to have any legs. It began to look like an athletics discus, rolling towards him, upright upon its edge.

The disc reached his feet and began to run up the leg of his jeans. It was trailing a strip of yellow tape, which stuck to everything behind it. The tape stretched from his jeans all the way back along the wire to where Zert was working away at his communicator on the other side of the gulf. Suddenly there was a click and the disc began to run backwards, taking in the tape as it went. It dropped off his leg and stopped on the wire. Awg could see that Zert was waving his arms about, obviously trying to say something. Gingerly, Awg lifted one foot off the cable. At once, the disc ran forward a few inches to his other foot. Awg swapped feet, stepping over the disc, which then ran on as far as the cliff. And then vertically up it to the top.

Awg could not see what it did next. He discovered a few minutes later that the disc had run around at the top, winding the tape around rocks, trees, and any obstacle it could find. The next thing that Awg saw was the *other* end of the tape coming towards him. It had detached itself from the point where Zert was working and was now unzipping itself along the wire until it hung loose down into the canyon. It then began reeling in from Awg's end of the wire and gathering itself into loops and folds up and down the eight foot drop between the cable and the top of the cliff. Awg waited until it had finished and become quite still, and then gave a few experimental tugs on the loops hanging down towards him. Whatever was sticking them together was doing a good job, and, by using the loops as hand- and foot-holds, he managed to climb.

The man in the tweed jacket reached down, grabbed his hand and hauled him over the top.

'I've never seen anything like that in all my born days,' he said. 'Which circus are you from? Or are *you* not from Earth, either?'

Awg was desperate to talk. To ask questions. But he was remembering Flossie and what had happened to her. It was a warning. Even when he'd got off the wire, the danger wasn't over.

Fifty Two

They heard the sound of the engines first, out of sight, on the steep side of the hill. First softly, then louder, then more softly again. Circling, checking out the wreck of Asa's plane, searching, searching. Then the two transporters roared into view from over the brow and immediately bore straight down upon them. Awg and his companion both dived for cover. The old man was surprisingly quick on his feet. Awg could see that his face was cut and bruised.

The planes circled for what seemed ages before disappearing over the other side of the hill. Awg began to breathe more easily. Perhaps they hadn't been spotted after all. Or perhaps they had, and the transporters would soon be back. Or were out of sight, waiting …

Awg's head was full of questions, but one thing stood out above all the others.

'What happened to Asa?' he asked urgently. 'Is she alive?'

The old man looked anxiously at the sky, then at Awg.

'She's trapped in the plane. I couldn't get her out. And now the hillside's on fire. We've got to be quick.'

He led the way over the hilltop to where they could look down on the wrecked transporter. The wheeled undercarriage was burning fiercely and flames were spreading rapidly up the hill. Very soon they would reach the rest of the plane where it lay pinioned by the trees. The old man again scanned the sky. For the present, it was empty.

As they hurried down, Awg battled to keep his mind focused on the task before them. But all the time, his personal anguish threatened to overwhelm him. He had to know.

'Is your name Joseph?' he asked, hardly able to get the words out. The lump in his throat felt so huge he thought he would choke.

'Yes – but how ... ?'

Awg was near to tears. He ached with longing to talk to this man he knew so much about but had never met – and for years had believed it was impossible to meet. He needed hours, days – not seconds.

'Asa told me on the radio,' he said, untruthfully.

By the time they reached the cabin section of the helicar, they could feel the waves of heat beating towards them from the burning hillside. Awg clambered up into the dome and was shocked to see the damage. As Joseph followed, Awg wondered how he had escaped with so little injury. Asa was lying in the pilot's seat with the control column smashed down on top of her. She was breathing but unconscious. Awg knew she probably shouldn't be moved but they had no alternative.

Between them, Awg and Joseph tried in vain to bend the control column away from Asa and back towards its proper position.

'What about the seat?' shouted Joseph. 'If those controls can't be moved, perhaps we can shift that.'

Awg found four clamps under the seat and although they were very stiff he managed to get them undone. They each grabbed one side of the seat and with some hefty thumps got it to slide backwards for about a foot – enough to get Asa out. Awg was about to unbuckle her safety harness when Joseph stopped him. Instead, he took a penknife from his pocket and cut the harness away from its moorings in the cabin floor. He could see they were going to need it.

The flames were now only a few yards away. The smoke was billowing into the cabin and making them cough.

As gently as he could, Joseph lifted Asa across to the door. Awg jumped to the ground and Joseph lowered her down towards him, using the straps on her harness. At arms' length he had to let go and Awg lost his balance as he broke the last few feet of her fall. He was bruised and winded but hoped that he had saved Asa from harm. Joseph clambered down and with Awg's help managed to hoist Asa over his shoulder. They staggered off up the hillside, knowing they had to get as much distance as possible between themselves and the transporter. Its dome had now caught alight. Flames were licking up towards the rotor and the inside of the cabin was ablaze.

Awg wondered where the fuel tanks were. His question was answered by an explosion and blast of heat which threw them to the ground. The cabin where they had been such a short time ago was now a blazing fireball. They got up and struggled on towards the top of the hill.

'Where are we going to take her?' shouted Joseph. 'She can't go back the way you came.'

'No, but we've got to get to where my friends'll see us. I'm just hoping that they can do something.' Awg was wondering if their own transporter would fly again. Perhaps it was too badly damaged.

Eventually they reached the summit of the hill. On the far side of the ravine where Awg and his companions had landed there were now two other transporters and a crowd of people. It was easy to pick out Zert and Berjga. They were in the centre, surrounded by a ring of zwnerba guards.

Fifty Three

Awg and Joseph sank down out of sight.

'Those must be the planes that attacked us,' said Joseph, laying Asa down as gently as he could.

'Is that how you crashed?' asked Awg.

Joseph nodded. 'We were on our way from the place with all those aerial masts – and suddenly two other planes came towards us. There was a blinding green light and somehow we were blown completely off course. One moment we were flying over the desert and the next we were hurtling towards this hillside.'

Awg thought about the plasma cannon in their own attack and knew exactly what had happened.

'Somehow Asa managed to pull us around but it was too late. We crashed into those trees and the plane broke in two. I don't know what happened to the other aircraft. We never saw them again.'

But we did, thought Awg. And they're history. So they're definitely *not* the ones over there. Those are the new ones that buzzed us a minute ago.

He decided to take another look.

Awg could scarcely believe his eyes. Zert appeared to be helping to unload equipment from one of the transporters, while Berjga was sitting on a rock next to another zwnerba. They were talking together and helping themselves to food out of a large tin.

He crept back to where Joseph was sitting with Asa. She had her eyes open, and tried to raise her hand when she saw Awg. A trace of a smile creased her cheek, furrowing its way through the grime and clots of blood. She breathed a few words but only Awg heard and understood them. He knelt down at her side and spoke softly.

'No, you haven't failed. You haven't failed at all. I think we're all going to be OK.'

Leaving Joseph with Asa for a moment, he stood on the brow of the hill and shouted and ROARED and waved and jumped up and down until he was seen.

In less than five minutes they were being winched up into one of the hovering transporters, and in less than ten were on their way back to Auyvhasdh.

*

Asa was on a stretcher at the back of the plane; Berjga was with her. Awg was sitting with Joseph. Zert leant over from the seat behind.

'Diddya like the tape?'

Awg grinned. 'It scared me at first – but then I guessed it was another of your gadgets.'

'Yeah. Sentient tape. 's a bit basic at the moment, though. Besides movement, there's only four commands: *stick/unstick* an' *self/other*, so it's hard to control.'

Joseph laughed. 'When it came over the top I had to really dodge about to keep out of it's way. Otherwise I'd have been wrapped up like a Christmas parcel!'

'Zert,' said Awg. 'How did you do it?'

They both knew he wasn't talking about the tape. Awg was sure that their rescue must be due to Zert.

'Hard,' said Zert. 'Very hard. Not knowin'.

'The way I figured it out was like this. Xurog's th'only one can send help. But I can't be sure I c'n trust him. So what to do? If we don' get help, Asa's dead for sure, even if she ain't already. An' we're all likely to join her.

'So I called Xurog.'

'What – you spoke to him directly?' said Awg.

'Yep. I set him a test. Just think o' that: little trainee-technician Zert sets the Boss a test. An' it's not just any boss. He's like Head o' the City, Head o' the College an' Chief Spyridi advisor to the Patrician, all rolled into one. They don't come no bigger – or smarter.

'I tells him most o' the truth, at first. I tells him we – you an' me – stowed away in the transporter. An' that the zwnerba guards parachuted out. An' that we found the bomb an' chucked it overboard. AN' that we was attacked by two other planes AN' that we saw 'em off. So far so good. I reckoned if it was him that had planned it all, he'd know I was tellin' the truth.'

Awg looked on in amazement as Zert continued:

'But then, I bent it a little bit. I told him we'd rescued Asa an' was all together in the plane an' still airborne but we'd got an unexploded shell stuck underneath. I asked him how to make it safe. Then I give him the codes I got off the transporter that attacked us, when I hacked into the firin' sequence for their third rocket. I give him six codes, three that disarmed it an' three that fired it. I asked him to tell me the ones that made it safe.

'I figured if he wanted rid of us all in one go, here's the perfect opportunity. He gives us the wrong codes an' Boom! – we're all little bits an' it was all the fault o' the hit men who'd fired at us, even if their shell took a while to go off.'

'And?' gasped Awg.

'He gave the right codes – all three. The chances o' that happenin' by accident are 20 to 1 against, so I reckoned Xurog was OK.'

'So – what then?'

'I confessed. I told him what I'd done an' that I was ready to carry the can for it. But please would he send help for Asa – an' you, o' course.

'So when we get back it's gonna be ex-trainee-technician Zert lookin' for a job. I'll prob'ly be sent to Hano to keep a watch on the lava pools. Endless years o' glurp glurp. Ugh!'

He sidled off and sat in a miserable heap at the back of the plane.

*

'You haven't told me your name,' said Joseph.

'Just call me Awg.' said Awg.

'You know,' said Joseph, 'it's a funny thing, but you do remind me of my son Thomas. You're much less dreamy but you do somehow look like him. He's an inventor.'

'Yes,' said Awg. 'I know.'

'He's got a little boy of his own now, although I haven't seen him since soon after he was born. He must be three years old now, I suppose.'

'Yes,' said Awg. 'I suppose he must.'

Fifty Four

'I just don't know what to do,' said Awg. 'However he got here, it's taken him ten Earth years to do it.'

They were sitting in the quiet courtyard at the back of Benedict's house. Joseph was inside, still asleep.

'I wonder how he *did* get here?' said Benedict, his chin in his hands. 'Three visitors from the same planet, and we have all travelled at different times from more or less the same place. There is certainly something very special about Llangarreg!'

'I'm sure it was that rock,' said Awg. 'We know it's one of the spyridi's beacons and he was sitting right on top of it.'

'Perhaps he got caught up in the sweep. Every few months they send out a large pulse of power to keep all the beacons active. It's a beam of energy that sweeps around the Universe.'

'Around *Zero's* universe, you mean.'

'Yes, but it must be able to penetrate Earth's universe too, or the beacons there wouldn't work.'

'Does this beam go out from that communications place at Chykideyh, where they found him?' asked Awg.

'Yes, that is where they transmit the beam and receive the incoming signals.' A look of bewilderment was apparent on the monk's face. 'I wish I knew more about such things – but I thought that the equipment at Chykideyh was quite different from that used for matter transportation. The two things should be completely separate.'

'Xurog told me the plasma transport system "stores" stuff in Earth's universe before it finally gets sent off.'

'Then maybe,' said Benedict, 'the two sorts of beams can

sometimes get mixed up.'

'Perhaps that explains the delay!' said Awg. 'Joseph disappeared when I was three years old and he's only just arrived here on Zero.'

He got up and wandered in small circles around Benedict's seat.

'Do you think he was "suspended"? Zert told me that people can get stuck, where they've disappeared from one place but haven't got where they were going to.'

'Possibly,' replied Benedict, 'but my understanding is that there is no definite link between time in this Universe and that in Earth's – that time trundles on independently in the two worlds. From my own experience, the only rule I've discovered is that time always goes forwards. When you come back, it's always at a later time than when you left. But it could be a minute after, or two hundred years later. It's all very perplexing.'

'But what are we going to tell him?' said Awg, in an agonised voice. 'That not only has he already been away from Earth for ten years, but there's no way to get back? He's not a young man. The shock might kill him.'

'I think there is only one thing to do,' said Benedict, 'and that is to tell him the truth. Gently, and perhaps not all at once. I believe he is a lot tougher than you think. Look at the way he worked with you to rescue Asa. From what you say, you would never have got her out of the burning transporter and away to safety if it had not been for him.'

'No, that's true. He was wonderful. And he didn't panic at all. He was dead calm.'

*

Joseph awoke in a cold sweat. He'd been dreaming. He was back in the war: a navigator, flying over Germany in a Wellington bomber. They'd just been shot at by a Messerschmitt Bf 109. Apparently no damage, and they'd shaken the Jerry off. Just to be sure, he'd crawled back to see that Jimmy was OK. Jimmy was the rear gunner – in those old Wimpey bombers, horribly exposed. Joseph remembered it all like it was yesterday. At the back of the plane, there were armoured doors to stop bullets reaching the rest of the crew. On his knees, he'd opened them. And there was his mate Jimmy Gibson – or what was left of him – smeared over the blood-spattered Perspex of his turret. Then the 109 came back, and brought his friends with him. Joseph's starboard engine was shot to bits and they crashed in a field just north of Düsseldorf.

That flight in the transporter had brought it all back. The noise of the aircraft, the fear at the attack. Going down. Smashing into the hillside. The jarring, mind-numbing impact of the crash. The acrid, choking smoke. And the terror of wondering how long it would be before the fuel tanks went up.

The other stuff had been quite tame after that. Sure, it was a shock to be confronted by eight-foot tall creatures with silvery skins and such like. But compared to seeing your best friend gunned into a bleeding pulp ...

He didn't know how he'd got here, or where he was, but the important thing was to get back again, to get home. How long had he been gone? Three nights? Four? Annie would be worried out of her mind.

The boy would help. He seemed a good lad and to know his way about. He would help. And that spider-being. He was clever, damned clever.

And as for that monk. That had been another shock, him turning up as well. Nothing else would surprise him now.

There was a knock at the door. After a pause, Benedict came in. They chatted. Joseph was surprised. Then they had a long discussion about clocks.

*

Awg and Joseph went to visit Asa. She still looked a mess but was very glad to see them. They were told that she was going to be all right. The concussion and broken ribs were the worst damage. Her carers thought she would be allowed to get up in about a week or so.

On the way back, Awg started the conversation he had been dreading.

'Did Benedict tell you how we got here – about matter transport?' he asked.

'Benedict told me a lot of things,' replied his grandfather. 'The whole business is quite extraordinary. People being whisked through space as if they were changing from one scene to the next in a film. I don't know whether to believe it or not. I suppose I've got to. You don't get green moons or talking spiders on Earth – at least as far as I know.'

Joseph laughed uneasily. He spread out his hands, looking down at them as if to check that they, at least, were real.

'And we all came from Llangarreg! But why were you in my house? – and what was Annie thinking about, letting a visitor tamper with one of my clocks!'

Awg decided to try a different approach.

'Joseph – what do you know about Benedict?'

'He said he was the one who made the clocks – and he certainly knew everything about them. I suppose he meant he was a descendent with the same name.'

'But what if he meant it literally – that he was actually the same person?'

'It's impossible. That clock was made in the late eighteenth century. He would have to be over two hundred years old!'

'But how else could he know so much detail about the clocks?' said Awg. 'And monks don't have children – or at least, not usually.'

'Then how do you explain it?'

'Only by saying that it's true. He *is* the Benedict who founded the workshop in Llangarreg. As a matter of fact, he was actually born in the year 1361 and he lived in the monastery when it was working and hadn't been pulled down yet.'

'Don't be ridiculous!'

'Not so long ago, you wouldn't have believed that a monk

could travel through space. Just say for a moment that it's all true; that time on the Earth and time here are not the same.

'Look at me, Joseph, and think who I might be – who I am. Think why I was at Bryn Castell, why I love your Annie so much, why I could tell you every detail about your workshop, and about your son Thomas and where he lives and what he does.

'Ten years have passed on Earth since you vanished from the top of Gellyn mountain – and I am your grandson.'

Fifty Five

Awg slept soundly that night. He had spent all the rest of the day with Joseph. They had laughed together, cried together, and talked until they were both exhausted. It had been one of the most wonderful times of his life.

But next morning, and all too early, Awg was woken by a thumping on his door and got up to find Zert outside. He was shaking from head to foot.

'You gotta come with me. Now. The P-P-Patrician wants to see us.'

Awg rubbed his eyes and tried to make sense of the words.

'But it's a long way to Gexadkydubm and I'm not even properly awake yet.'

'No. No. You don' understand. He's *here* – in Auyvhasdh. We gotta report to the Great Hall at college. All of us. NOW.'

They ran over to Benedict's house and collected Awg's grandfather. It was still very early and there was no one else about. They passed like ghosts through the deserted streets.

They entered the Great Hall and its huge doors were closed behind them. The vast space stood silent, waiting. The three adventurers moved hesitantly out of the shadows and began to walk down the broad central aisle between the empty rows of carved wooden benches. Their footsteps rang out on the stone floor, echoing up to the vaulted ceiling. Feeling as small as ants, they came to a halt in the circle of light at the front of the hall.

Seated in the tall ceremonial chairs at each side were Xurog and the Director of the Records Office. In the centre, red-robed, was the Patrician himself. Before them stood Awg, in jeans and a tee-shirt, his hair like a black haystack; Joseph, in his tweed jacket and grey flannels, wondering what it was all about; and Zert, hopping from one limb to another and scared out of his wits.

Each of them felt that the eyes of the Patrician were on him alone. The frail old man seemed somehow larger than even Xurog himself, and his presence pervaded the great chamber. His voice broke the silence like the sudden cracking of ice.

'I address myself to you who stand before me: to our visitors from planet Earth – the boy known as Awg and his grandfather – and to you, trainee-technician Zertalan Baskuborok.'

At the mention of his name, Zert looked as if he were about to die on the spot.

'I have spoken with my daughter. Through your brave actions, her life has been spared. I am assured that she will make a full recovery – as also will Berjga, her pilot.'

Awg looked up sharply. What was the Patrician saying? Berjga, *her pilot*? He listened even more intently as the old man continued.

'It was indeed fortunate that you yourselves were not caught in the dust storm which brought down Asa's transporter.'

Dust storm? What was all this stuff? Awg fixed his eyes on Xurog, who looked on impassively. Awg cast a swift glance around. His grandfather looked as baffled as he was, while Zert was still petrified by being in the same room as the Patrician. No one was going to say anything.

Suddenly Awg saw it all. Weakened by her injuries, Asa had taken the easy way out. Probably she had tried to tell her father the truth – with the usual negative result. So she had caved in and resorted to this fable of crashing in a dust storm.

Awg was furious. Sooner or later, someone had to prick the bubble of the Patrician's golden fantasy world. He watched as the Ruler of Zero spoke again – and his anger died away as he realised the stubborn old man's obvious sincerity.

'I offer you my heartfelt thanks – and I wish to repay you for your sacrifices. First, I will deal with the member of our own community.' His gaze fell on Zert, who was trembling so much he could hardly stand.

'I am told that you doubted the loyalty of Xurog, the Master of this City, and withheld information from him until you were sure he would not harm my daughter. Is this true?'

'Y – Y – Y – Y – Y – Y – Yes.'

'I am also told that you tried out various experimental inventions, not knowing if they would work or not. You held many lives in the balance. What would you have done if your devices had failed?'

'I – I – I – I suppose I'd have tried to th – th – think of something better ...' stammered Zert.

'So, even in great danger, you would not have given up attempting to save your friends?'

'N – N – No. N – N – Never.'

'And for how long have you served your apprenticeship?'

'F – Four years.'

'And how much longer do you need to serve?

'Th – Three y – years.'

'Then Xurog has asked me to give you this. Come forward and take it.'

Zert tottered up to the Patrician's seat, bowed, and took a large scroll from his hand. As he turned to rejoin the others, he could not see the ghost of a smile on the Patrician's face.

'And now,' continued the Patrician, 'I turn to those who have come to us across time and space. Your arrival may have been unexpected, but your presence here and your courageous actions have prevented a terrible calamity. In recognition of our debt, I offer you anything which it is in my power to give. You have only to ask.'

Awg was aware that he was in the presence of a great statesman, and could only imagine the power and riches that he was even now, in his decline, able to command. He remembered Asa's words about the abundance of gold and diamonds on Zero. But Awg knew that he wished for none of it.

'We are proud and glad to have been of service to you,' replied Awg. 'But there's only one thing I want now, and it seems that it is in no one's power to give. I wish only to go back to my home and return my grandfather to his family.'

The Patrician looked solemn, and infinitely sad. 'I regret that you are indeed correct,' he said. 'What you desire is beyond us. But surely, is there nothing else?'

'No, thank you,' said Awg. 'Your people have shown us great generosity and kindness and we ask for nothing more.'

Joseph, who was rather overcome, nodded vigorously. Awg bowed, and with the others was about to leave. But, after a few steps, he halted. Marooned on Zero, he had little to lose. Perhaps here was a chance – slender, but never to be repeated – to make that world, at least, a better place. He turned to face the Patrician once more.

'Your Honour, there is one thing – but it may anger you that I ask it.'

Whatever he may have thought or anticipated, the Patrician betrayed no sign of emotion.

'You may make your request.'

'When we last met, you asked me if I was a messenger – and I replied, truthfully as I thought then, that I was not. But now I realise that perhaps I do have a message after all – and my request is that you give me the chance to speak with you again – soon – and tell you what it is.'

Fifty Six

The Patrician was silent for a while, but then a strange expression spread across his face – a look of apprehension, but within it something almost of relief.

'Speak *now*, if you do not fear to do so,' he said. 'Perhaps your message should be heard by more than myself alone. Do you accept this?'

'Yes,' said Awg, fighting to keep his voice steady.

'Then begin.'

There was a silence so total that breaking it seemed an impossibility. Awg took a very deep breath. The enormity of what he was about to do overwhelmed him. He had been entrusted with the innermost secrets of others. What right had he to reveal them? Was it a hammer blow for justice – or a colossal betrayal? He wondered if he might be signing his own death warrant – and even, perhaps, that of others.

The seconds ticked away, and, with every second, the silence grew heavier and Awg more desperate. He'd made a terrible mistake. He should say nothing. What chance had he of making any impression where the Patrician's own daughter herself had failed? How was he even to begin? He imagined himself back in his first meeting with the Patrician and struggled to find the right connection with what he now wanted to say.

And, at last, he found it.

And when he had found it he knew it was right. And so, when he started to speak, his voice was clear and confident and he was no longer afraid.

'Your honour – at our last meeting, you spoke to me of the

oath you swore on becoming Patrician of Zero. You told me how you made a solemn promise to dedicate your life to the service of Zero and its Galaxy. I will now swear to you in the same spirit:

I swear to work for the good of Zero and its people
to strive for truth and fairness in all my actions
and to seek no personal reward.

The Patrician's eyes never left Awg's face as he spoke the ceremonial lines. They were the menacing grey of an angry sea. Awg felt as if a dark searchlight had been focused upon him.

'In this action you have made a most serious pledge,' said the old man grimly, 'and you will be held to it. Now you must prove that these are not empty words.'

Awg closed his eyes for a second. He saw a picture of Asa, trapped in the cabin of her burning transporter.

'My message is this. You have told me of the threat to your planet from your dying sun – the mounting heat and the lack of water. But there is another threat that you do not wish to recognise. The very truth and fairness of which you are justly proud is itself dying.

'It was no dust storm that brought down Asa's plane. It was the actions of her enemies – her enemies, and yours. We ourselves were attacked on our way to rescue her. It was only Zert that saved us.

'Asa has recognised the decay of your society and has fought against it. She has herself truly served Zero and its Galaxy and has nearly paid for her dedication with her life. It is she and her brave comrades who have worked tirelessly for truth.'

The Patrician turned on Awg in his anger.

'Truth! How can this be the *truth*! Who are you? An accidental traveller who has been here for hardly a moment of time. You understand nothing of our tradition. What do you know about *truth*?'

'It is the truth because he has no reason to lie.'

The voice came from high in the gallery above them. Everyone looked up. Asa stood at the front of the balcony in a white hospital coat.

'And it is the truth because he is honest and has sworn to you that it is so.'

And now an astonishing change transformed their surroundings. No one had realised that Zert was missing. As Awg had been speaking he had slipped away to the back of the Hall.

They were plunged into darkness, and it seemed to Awg that he was once again in Mayor Sharibvdl's hideous office. Everything was there: the garishly coloured walls, the bulbous statues, the huge purple desk. And in the desk sat Sharibvdl. And talking with him was – Awg himself.

Those gathered in the chamber were witnessing a complete re-creation of that day in Gexadkydubm. Awg watched in amazement. When Zert said that he had recorded the conversation, Awg had not thought in terms of spyridi technology. Sharibvdl's words echoed through the Hall:

> 'Welcome to our humble province. It is *such* an honour ...'
> 'This GRAN – is she a relative of the QUEEN you spoke of? From whom perhaps you derive your own royal ancestry and wealth ...'
> 'I discovered some simple rules. The first is, walk over anyone who is no use to you. On the other hand, cultivate those who can advance your career ...'
> 'Now I've got to the top, I do exactly as I like ... fixing contracts and siphoning off the money into my own companies. No one can touch me because they know I'll get them drawn into prison ...'
> 'What higher authorities? The Patricians? That's a laugh. The old families're finished. Washed up. They'd better look out. Soon it'll be New-Patrician Sharibvdl and his family ...'

'Look on! See for yourselves the poison that is abroad! And what you witness here is only a tiny fraction of the whole.'

This time it was not Asa who spoke. At her side stood a tall young Zeroian.

'Now look again! Look at those who are fighting alongside your true and faithful daughter for all the things you say you hold dear. Fighting – and paying with their lives!'

A new scene surrounded them. They were underwater, swimming along a deep channel. Now to the surface, breaking out into a large circular chamber.

The light beam above the headlamp camera sweeps around the space. There is a dark pool, its rocky walls glistening with condensation. Three black pipes disappear upwards from the central cistern. Two figures are sprawled out on a narrow ledge. The camera goes towards them, closer and closer until the field of view is filled by their young faces – faces which are blotched, purple, and lifeless.

K2 never forgot the look on the Patrician's own face at that moment. A face staring up at him, lit in the brilliance of the projected image. A face no longer proud, haughty and magisterial, but haggard and deathly white with shock, horror – and guilt.

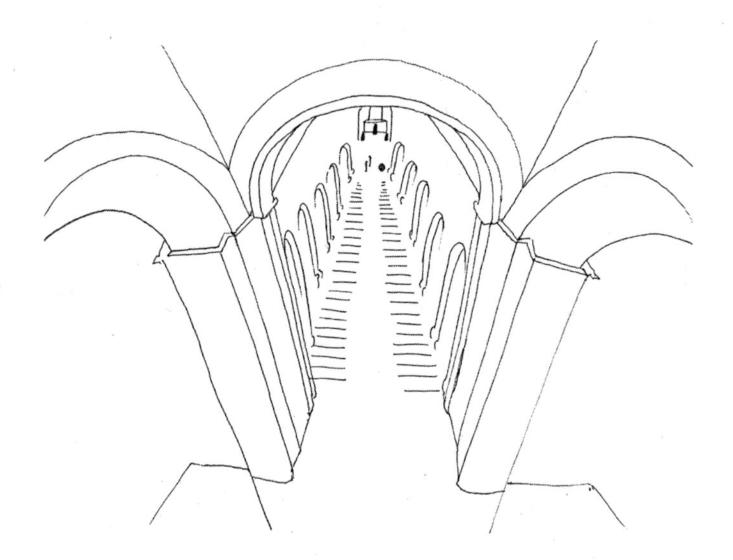

Fifty Seven

'Jus' look at it!' cried Zert, waving the scroll in the air. 'It's my Technician's Certificate. An' it's signed by Xurog *an'* the Patrician. I bet *nobody, ever's* got one like this.'

'So does that mean you've finished being a trainee?' asked Awg.

'Well, sort of,' said Zert. 'But 'tween you an' me I had to promise Xurog I'll attend the rest o' the classes. It's fair, 'cos I do need to know all that stuff.'

'Do you reckon life's going to carry on like before, then?'

'Can't tell. Depends on the way the Patrician reacts, an' how quick. Asa's the key, o' course. She got so much stuff to tell him, an' no one knows if he's gonna take it on board.'

'It's different for me,' said Awg. 'I just feel, like – in the way, now. Lots of things are going to change, and I can see I'm not part of them any more.'

'To be honest,' confided Zert, 'when you showed up there was a sort o' expectation you'd bring along somethin' new – like Benedict did. New discov'ries. Not like this. No one knows what'll happen now.'

'If it all goes pear shaped, I'll probably end up as Public Enemy No.1,' replied Awg gloomily.

'No you won't. You'll get forgotten 'bout for a bit 'cos you've rocked the boat an' they don' like that. But that'll change. I reckon you'll be famous one day. P'raps they'll put up a statue.'

'Well, I suppose it's better than ending up in the Hall of Memory!'

'Don't say that. It's that sort of stuff I really come about. I bin thinkin.'

Awg looked up. 'About what?' he said.

'Bout how you got here. I hacked into the system at Tukzadryk an' got out all the data 'bout your auto-extradition. Component unit number, field strength, beam density, arrival time – I got all of it.'

'So?'

'You know Benedict told you 'bout the guys they sent off into the Dark Universe, tryin' to get to your planet?'

'The ones that got killed?'

'Yep – 'cept they didn' actually get killed – not as far as we know, anyhow – they got lost. An' the reason they got lost is that the people at this end didn' have enough data to send 'em safely – that is, with a fair guarantee they'd end up where they wanted to go.

'The way plasma transport works is by coordinates – you specify exact time an' place o' departure an' exact place o' destination. An' o' course they didn' know much 'bout the destination, so they had to make the best guess they could – an' obviously it warn't good enough.

'Now, there's another way o' settin' the coordinates, an' that's to let the system work it out for itself. But for that you needs *objects*. Objects an' times. The object sets the location an' the time gives the distance. That's one o' the ways they does the short, routine transfers – like to Hano. That's the nearest inhabited planet to Zero.'

'Where the lava pools are?'

'You gottit! They gives you a metal token: that's the *object*. But on the token they imprints a matrix givin' the time component o' your transfer. So, later, youc'n use the token to get you back home. It'll take you to th'exact same place on Zero you started from. The token carries the info an' the transfer system can read it.

'Genr'lly speakin', the more data you got, the more likely your transfer'll work. So what I bin thinkin' is this. We already got a stack o' *arrival* data 'bout your trip – from the Tukzadryk log. If you got any way o' gettin' any *departure* stuff, we might have a chance o' sendin' you back. You gotta have some object that was there just as your transfer began, an' some way o' measurin' the time difference.'

Awg had begun to get excited, but now the whole thing seemed as hopeless as ever. Then he remembered the screwdriver.

'I was trying to open the power unit in the clock with a tool called a screwdriver – and when I woke up in prison I was still holding it. I've still got it. It's back in my room.'

He raced back to get it. He'd kept all his stuff in the brown box under his bed. He flipped it open, and there was the screwdriver. And then his heart missed a beat, because beside the screwdriver was his watch. He'd taken it off in Gexadkydubm in case it attracted attention. No one else wore anything like it so it was bound to be noticed. He'd almost forgotten about it. With shaking hands he picked it up. It was still working. He couldn't remember when he last put a new battery in.

He ran all the way back to Zert's room.

'Here's the screwdriver – and here's my watch.'

Zert looked at it with interest.

'Wossat?'

Awg explained.

'You mean to say people on your planet carries these around jus' to find out how much time has passed? Weird. So this small rod travels all round twice in one o' your Earth days. An' how d'you know how many days?'

Awg pointed to the little window where the date showed.

Now *Zert* was getting excited.

'We can use this! You say this device has run all the time you bin here, an' it was workin' when your transfer started?'

'Yes.'

'So, whatever time frame your journey took you through, this ...'

'Watch,' said Awg.

'... this watch has measured it. OK, so what's the exact time difference between when your transfer started an' now?'

Awg searched his memory. It was Thursday, August 2nd and his gran had caught the 10.30 bus down to Pontrhyd. It seemed just too fantastic to even *think* back to that day in Wales. By the time he had got the back off the clock and got to the power unit it would have been about half past twelve. And his watch now said 4.20 on the 24th. The date didn't have a black square around, so it was 4.20 pm.

'I think,' he said, 'in Earth time it's 22 days, 3 hours and 50 minutes.'

Zert grabbed the watch.

'OK, now I'll do some tests on it so I knows what it measures in units I'm used to.'

'Do you think there's a chance you can make it work for us?' asked Awg anxiously.

'Us? Who's *us?*' said Zert.

'Grandad and me.'

'Give us a break! It's gonna damage my brain to work all this out for one person. There's no way I can do it for two. Besides, all the calibration data's for you. Your grandad travelled from a different place at a different time. There's nothin' to tie his information to yours.'

Awg was aghast. He thought of his gran at Llangarreg.

'It's both of us, or nothing,' he said. 'I'm not going back without him.'

'What if ...' Awg's mind went racing back to the day he re-enacted his grandad's disappearance.

'What if I can tell you the exact time he started his journey and give you an object that was at the same spot?'

Zert clicked thoughtfully. 'That'd certainly make a difference – but it's still supermighty difficult.'

Awg tore back to his room again and ferreted about furiously in the brown box. He ran back to Zert and handed him the stone he'd picked up from the rock cairn on Gellyn mountain. So when had he put it in his pocket? Grandad had vanished at 11.15. They had arrived at 11 o'clock, so he had picked up the stone at about 11.03. They had made the journey on the Monday before he had worked on the clock.

'Zert – this stone was picked up 3 days, 1 hour and 27 minutes before I started my journey, and my grandfather began his journey from the exact same spot 9 years, 364 days 23 hours and 48 minutes before that.'

'OK. That's jus' 'bout nailed it,' said Zert, wearily. 'I'll do my best. Holy Moly! The stuff I do for you guys!'

'Thanks, Zert,' said Awg. 'You really are a marvel.'

'Awg ...'

'Yes, Zert ...'

'You realises the risk?'

'Well, I know that the plasma transfer process is a bit dodgy.'

'No, it's worse. Even if I gets everythin' totally fixed, you only got 'bout an evens chance o' landin' up *anywhere near* your own time an' orig'nal startin' point. It's Dark World stuff – an' no one knows the rules.'

Awg's face fell.

'An' there's more ...' added Zert.

Awg began to feel very uneasy.

'You got 'bout a ninety-five percent probability o' survivin' the transfer, but your grandad's chances are only forty percent 'cos o' his age.'

Fifty Eight

Saying goodbye was a very strange experience.

More than anything else, Awg wanted to be home and to get his grandfather back to Llangarreg safely. But there was so much else to think about. He didn't want to leave his friends on Zero, especially Asa and Zert. Were they safe now? How much had Asa been able to tell her father, and what action would he take? What would Sharibvdl – and those in the shadows behind him – do when they learnt of the Patrician's awakening from his coma of self-delusion?

And then there was the peril of the journey itself. At best, it was a gamble. Where would they end up, and would they survive? His own risk was relatively small – but his grandad had a less than a fifty-fifty chance of getting through it. Still, they had discussed the danger and Joseph had accepted it.

There wasn't much to do in getting ready. Neither Awg nor his grandfather had many possessions to take. Zert was very subdued. He felt responsible for their journey, and, although Xurog had agreed to the attempt, it was clear that he considered it unwise. As the time for their departure approached, Zert found he could hardly speak at all. At the last, he squeezed Awg's hand and pressed a small black glass disc into it.

'I'll really miss you,' he whispered.

'Me too,' said Awg. 'When we got attacked with those rockets – that was really wild! And it was you that saved us.' They locked a variety of arms in a bristly embrace.

Asa spent an hour with Joseph. He came away with a deeper understanding of Zero and its galactic empire, but with an even greater admiration for Asa herself.

With Benedict, it was like saying farewell to an actor on stage and knowing that you might encounter him in the street afterwards.

'Do you think we'll meet again?' asked Awg.

'I hope so,' said Benedict, shaking his hand warmly, 'but who can tell? Who knows at what future time I might walk again in the Priory at Llangarreg? Perhaps its buildings will one day be made whole once more, and a new gathering of my brethren live there. Stranger things have been.'

'Well, if I make it back,' said Awg, 'I'll keep a good look out for you.'

It had been hard enough parting from Zert but now he had to say goodbye to Asa as well. He reminded her of his rescue from Tukzadryk. They could laugh about the balerids now, but encountering them in the desert was a very different matter. And as for that ointment ...

'If I'd stayed, I was hoping you might get me some flying lessons,' he said.

'Well, maybe,' said Asa, 'but you didn't do so badly without, from what Berjga has told me.'

Awg had so much he wanted to say, but he found he couldn't bring himself to talk about any of the important things. He knew he would never have the chance again – and also it might be among the last things he ever said to anybody.

'You know those pyramid buildings in Gexadkydubm?' he asked, at last. 'The ones with the flights of steps and the flat tops, like the Records Office.'

'Yes, of course.'

'Some people on Earth think there's a link between the ones we have – the ones the Mayans built in Central America – and visitors from outer space.'

'Well, now you know that it's true.'

'You mean this really is where they got the idea?'

'No, of course not! Their buildings were the ones that gave *us* the idea.'

'What!'

'We copied them. They're not very old, you know. The really ancient buildings in Gexadkydubm are the houses in the old city, and, of course, my father's palace.

'But when the Old Patrician – my grandfather – saw the images of those temples from our beacons, he really liked them. So when it was time to reconstruct some parts of the city, some of the buildings and the monuments in the parks were made in the same style. We've copied things from other planets, too.'

It was nearly time for their departure. Awg couldn't bear their friendship to end like this. He was desperate to say some of the things he really felt.

'I – I never expected to make this journey, Asa,' he said. 'But it's been the most wonderful thing in my whole life. And meeting you ... You're just amazing, fantastic. I'll always think about you, and remember you – always.'

'I'll not forget you, either,' she said. 'I owe my life to your courage. And if in future times you should talk of me with your grandfather, know that I did what I could to repay the debt.'

*

Awg and his grandfather were escorted to a building near the transporter arrival station. They entered the spherical chamber and were strapped into two bunks at its centre. Awg noticed that the bunks had been recently moved until they were very close together. Joseph seemed to be having some difficulty getting comfortable, and he twisted and turned before settling down on his back.

The double doors were closed and the lights turned off. It was cold. There was absolute silence. It was very much like being put into a tomb ... alive.

Awg lay very still. His grandfather reached over and grasped his hand.

They waited, and Awg began to feel very scared, afraid that he would never see his grandfather again. He gripped the hand very tightly.

Someone shone a blinding light into his eyes.

Someone else grabbed him by the feet and whirled him round and round.

Someone else hit him over the head with a blunt, heavy object.

At least, that's what it felt like.

Fifty Nine

When Awg woke up, he did not feel good. It was exactly how he remembered it from waking up in Tukzadryk: the zonking pain in his head, the parched mouth, his body one massive ache. What he didn't remember was the roaring noise in his ears. But it didn't sound right. It was muffled, like it was right inside his skull. He was scared. Perhaps something had gone wrong in his head. Perhaps a bit of his brain had got squished on the journey.

Then he remembered the translocution modules. He'd got so used to having them stuck in his ears that he'd forgotten all about them. With some difficulty, he got them out – and then almost wished he hadn't. The noise was deafening. But at least he knew it was outside his head.

He was lying on a cold stone floor. He felt around with his hands. No, a rough, rocky floor. The floor of a cave. He felt around again. There was no one near. He was alone.

There was a very faint light ahead. He crawled towards it. The roaring noise grew steadily louder. His hands began to feel clammy and the knees of his jeans were getting wet. Suddenly he slipped.

He slid down a slope of wet rock, first on his front, then tumbling over and over, until he slammed into something very hard and solid. A drenching spray of water was falling on him from all sides. It forced itself into his eyes and ears. Coughing and spluttering, he backed away up the slope until the cascade of spray was reduced to a gentle shower.

He huddled into a corner and scrabbled at his face with his hands until he could get his eyes open without blinking.

In front of him was a wall of falling water. Real, wet, cold, flowing water – something he'd not seen for weeks. Gradually, he realised that the light coming to him from outside was from the night sky. He crawled forward again until he could look up and to the side of the water curtain. Beyond the waterfall was a single white moon and a myriad of stars. Stars he recognised: Orion, the Plough.

Awg buried his head in his hands and sobbed with joy. He was home, and he was alive. He'd made it.

He could see no way off the ledge on which he'd landed and had no alternative but to return to his corner and wait for dawn. He curled into a ball and shivered.

Cold and wet though he was, the exhaustion of his journey forced him into a fitful sleep. When he woke again, it was light. He was horrified to see where he was. Only a single large rock had prevented him from sliding off the ledge and into the waterfall. He would have been swept into the foaming pool at its base and pounded to death in seconds. Is this what had happened to Joseph? Had he crossed the Universe only to drown on Earth?

Awg crept back up the slope, emerging into a dimly lit cave. This must have been where he had first arrived. There was still no sign of his grandfather. At the very back of the cave, where it should have been darkest, there was a beam of light. As Awg picked his way towards it, the beam broadened into an expanse of sky framed by a circle of rock. A rough scramble brought Awg to the opening, where he found himself at the bottom of a steep and stony track. After climbing for a while through trees, the path came out into open hillside.

Awg gazed wildly around, trying to get some idea of where he might be. He was desperate to find something made by man to give some idea of time. If Benedict's idea was right, he shouldn't have arrived in the Stone Age or in medieval times. But it could be at any time after the incident with the clock. Perhaps there would be super-evolved humans floating about in transparent bubbles. Perhaps there would be no humans at all.

But the landscape looked familiar. No scorched plains or a countryside withered by nuclear devastation. There were green fields and wooded hills. This was either central Wales or somewhere very much like it.

He stopped at a stile and looked across the valley – and saw two cottages at the end of a narrow lane. He saw the old forest road behind them. He could even see the stone bridge where the road divided, and, high above that, the graveyard of the old forest on the open hillside; and, still higher, the grassy ridge that led to the summit of Gellyn mountain.

With tears streaming down his face he tore down the path, stumbling over the stones and blundering over stiles, racing across the little fields towards the distant buildings. When he reached them, he stopped. He stared at the cottages, drinking in every detail. They weren't derelict, the roofs hadn't fallen in, there were still people living there. The doors were painted the same colour that he remembered. The tractor in the tiny barn was the same one he'd seen before.

Awg lost it completely, dancing around, screaming and shouting – until a window was thrown open and a woman in a red nightgown demanded to know what all the noise was about at six o'clock in the morning.

'Please, please,' he shouted. 'Please tell me what date it is. It's very important.'

'It is August 30th – and it is a Sunday – so will you please be respecting our peace and quiet and be taking yourself away this instant.'

Awg looked at his watch. It said that the date was the 30th.

'I'm sorry,' he shouted. 'I'm sorry. Thank you so much.'

Then he realised he'd forgotten to ask the year. Dare he disturb them again?

No, he didn't need to. He raced across to the tractor and looked up at the licence disc. It was dated the year he'd come to Llangarreg. He was in his own time.

*

Awg's grandmother was a very sensible and practical woman. She had her own opinions of the odd things that tended to happen in Llangarreg. She could see that most of them were either natural oddities or the workings of the over-active imaginations of gullible people. But there were some things that were Not Easily Explained.

When she saw her husband disappear into thin air, it was a terrible shock. She was heartbroken, but she never gave up hope. It was not as if he had died in a car accident, or anything like that. It was like those days in the war, when people went missing. You always feared the worst, but hoped for the best. Joseph's disappearance was Not Easily Explained. But what vanished one day might perhaps re-appear on another, especially in Llangarreg.

Ten years was a very long time to wait, and even Annie Bradley's resolve had been beginning to weaken. But Awg coming to stay had changed all that. Mrs Bradley was a believer in Providence, and if Providence had sent her Awg, then it might have other surprises in store.

So when she went upstairs to discover that Awg himself had disappeared and that there were bits of a clock scattered all over the floor, she knew that something very odd was afoot. He had not taken his anorak or rucksack or any food. She knew instinctively that whatever had happened to Joseph had now overtaken Awg as well and that the two events were somehow closely connected. She had harboured a suspicion for a long time that the old black clock was not just a harmless timepiece.

She loved her husband, and she had come to love Awg too. Something told her that if she was going to get them back, then the objects connected with their disappearance were important and could be used in some way. So she gathered up all the pieces of the clock mechanism, and its triangular case, and put them carefully away in a box.

On the 29th of August, she woke up in the night to find that all the lights in the house had come on. They stayed on for about a minute and then faded out. She checked the switches and they were all off. She went outside. There was a beautiful clear sky – and almost at once she saw a shooting star.

As soon as it was daylight, she took all the pieces of the clock out of the box and carried them up the mountain. There, she spread them out over the surface of the large white rock, sat down, and waited.

*

Awg left the cottages and trekked along the old forest road. He crossed the stone bridge and took the left fork through the trees. He climbed the track by the stream, passed the stone sheep pen and strode across the hillside with its wiry grass and stunted gorse bushes.

He skirted the dead tree tombstones, passed through the gate in the wire fence, and began to walk along the grassy ridge to the summit. Below him, the mountain sheep picked their way sure-footedly along their precipitous tracks. Awg remembered Flossie, and grinned to himself.

Earlier, he had begun to panic at finding no trace of his grandad. But now, the higher he climbed, the calmer he felt.

He came to the place where the medieval monks had cut the cross into the rock to mark the way. He thought of Benedict, with his gentle face and wistful smile.

The top of the mountain was almost in view.

In a few steps, Awg halted. Two old people were sitting on the white boulder with their arms around each other, and he didn't want to disturb them.

Sixty

The three of them walked back down the mountain together. No words were spoken.

As they passed the cottages, a woman came out to the gate, no longer in her red nightgown.

'It's out very early that you are, Mrs Bradley,' she called.

Then, seeing Awg, she added, 'I'd be very careful of that young man, if I were you. He's not quite right upstairs, if you take my meaning.'

Awg's gran smiled. 'It's all right, Mrs Pugh. He's had a trying time recently.'

'And who would your friend be, then?' asked Mrs Pugh, staring at Joseph.

'Oh, just someone I used to know, a long time ago.'

*

It took several days for Awg and Joseph to tell Awg's grandmother their story. Many of Awg's adventures were new to Joseph as well. They talked, and slept, and ate large and delicious meals together. Awg had forgotten what proper food tasted like – and he enjoyed finding out.

'Is all this really true?' asked Awg's grandmother. 'About you being in prison, and the spiders, and this girl Asa? And you and Joseph rescuing her?' She had been prepared for something out of the ordinary, but nothing as strange as the world of Zero.

'Every single word,' said Awg and Joseph together.

'Well, it's a good thing you've got me to tell it to, because you'll never be able to say a word to anyone else. They'd take you for a couple of lunatics and lock you away. Especially as you can't prove anything. It's not as if you've come back with a packet of photographs.'

Awg felt in his pocket and brought out Zert's glass disc. It hadn't disintegrated on the journey or become invisible on reaching Earth. Although Awg didn't know exactly what it was, he had a shrewd idea. He remembered the memorials in the Hall of Memory and held it to the light. Looking through from one side, he saw a three-dimensional picture of Asa; and from the other side, a picture of Zert. Without a word, he handed the glass to Joseph, who looked, nodded, and passed it on to Grandma Annie. There was a sharp intake of breath as she saw Asa, and then a little scream when she looked at Zert.

'Things will never be the same now, for any of us,' she said. 'We have a secret that we can't share with anyone else. When we look up at the stars, we'll know, for certain, that somewhere out there are people like us, and people not like us, and all manner of amazing and wonderful things. We'll be living our lives and they'll be living theirs, and only the three of us here will know.'

'I brought something back too,' said Joseph. 'I've kept it hidden until now because Asa told me to. It's a gift for Awg.'

Awg looked up in surprise, wondering what sort of thing Asa might have sent. A pot of that balerid ointment as a reminder, perhaps?

'She said I must keep it inside my coat, and not show it to you until we got safely home. And she said that when we started our journey, I was to get as close to you as possible and lodge the thing between the two of us. I don't know why. It was damned uncomfortable. Anyway, here it is.'

From inside his coat he produced a very strange object. It consisted of three bronze-coloured metallic spheres joined together by a silver rod. The central sphere was much larger than the outer ones and was about the size of a cricket ball.

Awg at last understood Asa's final words to him. She had indeed done what she could to repay the debt. She had sacrificed her own future security to save their lives and ensure that they reached Earth safely. He remembered the Director's words in the Patrician's palace. The iridonium resonator had taken their most skilled scientists three years to make; it was the only one of its kind; it was priceless.

His grandmother and grandfather looked on in alarm as Awg just stared and stared at Asa's gift, his jaw dropped open.

Eventually, his grandfather asked, 'Do you like it? Asa said it was something special.'

Awg didn't know what to say. *He* might have made it home safely, but it was unlikely that his grandfather would have survived the journey. Without this.

'I – I can't explain exactly what this is just at the moment. It's something very, very special. She sent it to help us on our journey.'

'Like a good luck token?' said his gran.

'Yes, that's it – a good luck token.'

Sixty One

Awg and his grandfather were up in the workshop, surrounded by clockmaker's tools, books, and the clean smell of wood shavings and machine oil. It seemed so wonderful to Awg that they should now be there together. He had spent many days and nights alone in that strange, round room. Everything had been a reminder of the grandfather that he had believed he would never see. Awg went quietly across to one of the tall windows and gazed out, first across the expanse of Wales, and then down upon the old chapel in the Priory. Zero seemed impossibly distant.

Joseph was looking though the box of pieces from the black clock.

'It's going to take while, but I think I'll manage it,' he said. 'In fact, I promised Benedict that I would.'

'Manage what?' said Awg, with interest.

'To rebuild the Old Curiosity.'

'You're not serious!'

'Oh yes, I think it would be a very appropriate project. Get me back into practice so that I can start making new clocks again.'

He gave a mischievous and rather guilty smile.

'Besides, otherwise I wouldn't have a home for this, and I can't leave it lying about. Someone might have an accident with it.'

From out of his pocket, he produced a small, flat cylinder of dull grey metal. On the side of the cylinder was a mark: a strange symbol, a bit like a child's drawing of the sun.

'Oh no!' cried Awg. 'You're not going to?'

'Why not? Benedict asked Zert to get it for me so that I could make a proper job of the restoration. With that clock in its place again, I shall feel things are really getting back to normal.

'And when you come and stay with us at Llangarreg – as I hope you will very often – there'll be one less job for you to do. It's good to have a clock you never have to wind.'

*

Awg was walking up the valley. He wanted to give his grandparents some time to themselves. They were together again. Of all that had happened, that was the best bit. It turned out that Joseph had been five years older than Annie when they married. Now she was five years older than he was. It didn't seem to matter. They were very happy. They'd certainly have plenty to talk about. Awg had been so focused on their time on Zero that he'd almost forgotten Joseph also had ten years of Llangarreg news to catch up on.

Awg walked up the valley to Ty Nant, to the cave behind the waterfall that he'd always been meaning to explore – but never had until he'd arrived back there by accident from another world. Then he retraced the journey he'd made on that never-to-be-forgotten morning: down to the cottages, up to the top of the mountain. He'd brought with him a white card on which he'd drawn, in waterproof pen, a picture of himself and Joseph and Grandma Annie. He fixed it to a bush, right by the white rock, but on the opposite side from the path and where few people would notice it. With a bit of luck, it might stay there long enough to register on the image the beacon was sending out. He wondered how many more beacons there were, and where. From now on he'd keep a look out for that tell-tale mark.

He went down to Llangarreg again and into the grounds of the Priory. Awg walked back to where the field path entered, and remembered how scary it had been on that first night – the night he had met Benedict. Entering the cool of the chapel, he left a note in the recess by the side of the altar. He hoped no one would come and throw it away. It might have to stay there a long time. All it said was *Dear Benedict, please tell Zert and Asa we're all OK and thank them for everything. Yours, Awg.*

Then he went back to his room and packed up his stuff. He'd kept the fabric bag that Berjga had given him, and in it he put the things he'd had with him on his journey, all except the screwdriver and the stone from the top of Gellyn mountain, which Zert had needed to keep. He wrapped up Zert's glass in tissue paper and put that in as well. He wondered about the resonator. But something told him that it should stay in Llangarreg, so in the end Grandpa Joseph made a case for it and it occupied a place of honour on one of the windowsills in his workshop.

Awg wasn't sure about the watch. It had played a very important part in his adventure. Should he put that somewhere special too?

No, it was just an ordinary watch, so he'd carry on using it every day as he'd always done.

It was just an ordinary watch that had been taken to pieces and then re-assembled by a rather clever trainee technician of the Spyridi.

Sixty Two

Awg got down from the train and looked along the platform. No one in sight. He hadn't really expected anyone to come and meet him – but all the same he felt mildly disappointed. It's not every day you come home from a different Universe.

When he got back, his mother was in the kitchen making some especially nutritious chicken broth for his father. She stared vacantly at Awg, then her face brightened.

'Oh hello, Allardyce. I wondered where you'd got to.'

'You sent me away.'

'Oh yes, I remember. You went off to stay with Granny Bradley. Did you have a nice time?'

'Uh – yes, thanks.'

'Your dear father's *so* much better and he's had this *wonderful* idea for an edible cereal bowl. Saves washing up after breakfast, you see. And, if you happen to run out of the cereal, you can just eat several of the bowls instead. Isn't that clever?

'They're made of reprocessed fish waste, so the taste needs a *little* bit of improvement, but he says it's only a matter of a tiny bit more development ...'

'I've done stuff, too,' said Awg.

'Yes, I'm sure. Fed the chickens, dug the garden, that sort of thing.'

'No, more than that.'

'Oh good. Some nature walks as well. A nice rest. But it must have been very dull. Well, what can you expect, stuck halfway up a mountain in the back of beyond? Nothing *ever* happens in those places.'

'And Mum …' said Awg.

'Yes, dear.'

'You know you told me that Gran had lost Grandpa.'

'Yes, dear. Very sad.'

'Well, she's found him again. He's come back.'

'That's nice. Now she won't be so lonely. Now Allardyce, dear, do run along – I've got to get your father his tea.'